SAME OLD SONG ©

C.L Hawkins

C.L Hawkins

<u>DEDICATION</u>

Father God, I thank you for giving me the strength and encouragement to follow my dreams. I've been writing since I was in High School. But when you hear others saying you can't do it you begin to believe it too. This is the time in my life to work on all of my dreams and make my daughters proud. Queen Tya and Princess Demi, thank you for coming into my life and growing with me. I hope you will be proud of Mommi.

To my wonderful parents and my brothers: thank you for always being here through all my downs falls and all my accomplishments. I just want y'all to be proud of me as well. I love you guys. Mr. Jaydee, I thank you and love you. My Enunu (P.R Rep) my sis-in-law thank you for everything.

Christina Santiago, you came into my life when it was all messed up. I watched you raise this beautiful young lady that goes by the name of C. Wilson. Let me tell you about your amazing daughter, she has been by my side through this whole ordeal. She has pushed me beyond my means. She has encouraged me to do better. Telling me, "Auntie, you got this" every day. Chris I know you're in heaven looking down at us and I hope that you're proud of your baby girl. Celeste I thank you for everything. I couldn't have done this without you.

To all my friends and family who have believed in me. I thank you guys as well for being in my ear saying "hurry the hell up with book, been hearing about this shit for years" I love you guys. Let me shout My Flatbush crews: Tennis Court, East 19th, East 18th, Ocean Ave, Regent St, Newkirk Ave, Tilden Ave, Beverly Rd, East 21st, Cortelyou Rd, Rogers Ave, Linden Ave, Parkside, Albemarle Rd, Martense, Caton Ave, St Paul, Clarkson Ave, Lenox Ave, Rutland Rd, Westbury, Winthrop, Hawthorne, Lott Ave.
FGK, FQT, UK, UQ, CMP, SMP, MOB, FBI, DECEPT, BMW, LO-LIFE, T-CLUB, STP, STEAM TEAM, VIP, FPK. Shout Out to My Brownsville Crew: ROROLIFE ENT.

Ok enough with mushy stuff. When I started this book I didn't know how it was gonna turn out. I had changed things up several times. Now that part one of *Same Old Song* is done and part two is in the making. My next book *D.O.C LOVE* will be dropping later on this year. I'm feeling more confident in myself.
IT'S GRIND TIME BAAABYY (in my IBRORO Voice). Now watch me work...
Look Out For the Flatbush Documentary

C.L Hawkins

Growing up in Flatbush, Brooklyn wasn't always fun but
if you lived on a well-known block people knew not to fuck
with you. The niggas on my block never got along with
nobody. Shit, they couldn't even walk one block up without
shots letting off. Tennis court was well known for the robbers
and shooters. You wanna know about the girls? Well they
were always was in some shit. There was one time they had a
cheering battle with these bitches from Regent Place and it
turn into a shootout. Twelve and thirteen year olds running for
their lives…
Aww the good old days…

Well, let me introduce you to Kim. Her mother, father, her
two brothers Quincy and Henry and her little sister Dominique
moved to Flatbush in the early 80's. She had to be like five
years old at the time. Quincy was the oldest, he was a terror,
and everybody was scared of that nigga. Henry, he was the
youngest brother, you can say he was the pretty boy but don't
get it twisted he would put your ass to bed. Their parents'
names were Maria and Luke. Maria was this gorgeous
Spanish Mamí. She resembled Claire from The Cosby Show.
She always kept her hair in a bun and she was always dressed
in the latest fashion.

Luke was an Afro American suave dude. He was a flashy
kind of guy that rode in the latest cars. He stayed fly from

head to toe. He was a part of the ultimate hustle. Luke was nothing to fuck with everybody respected him. No one was messing with the Shepherds.

1990

September 9th, the first day of school, Erasmus Hall was jammed pack; all the fly kids went there. This school is where you could find all the crews from different blocks like Clarkson, Lenox, Martense, East 21st, Westbury, Parkside, Crooke Ave, Beverly Road, Newkirk and of course Tennis Court. Everyone knew each other, some crews stuck with their own kind like those crazy ass Jamaicans from Martense Avenue or this Haitian crew who stayed in Polo from head to toe.

You see Kim and her girls stayed fly. They rocked Guess jean suits, fresh pairs of Stan Smiths and they all had their own unique look. Kim was 5'7 and thick but in all the right places. She was light skinned with chinky eyes. Her hair was down to the middle of her back. She stayed rocking two corn braids or a high ponytail. Her right hand's name was Tanya; she was a slim tall chick with dark skin. Everybody loved Tanya and wanted to get with her. She had this exotic look about her plus she was funny as hell. But she didn't care who wanted her because she was in love with Latrell. Latrell and Tanya had been together since Junior High School. He was a cool dude but he was always in some shit.

The last two of their click was Janay and Samantha. All of Kim's friends were dime pieces. All four of them rolled together since they were little kids. Now years later they were all in High School and were one of the most popular crews that Erasmus had to offer.

"Yo Kim I see we got most of the same classes." Tanya was so hype. Together all day was a good thing for her.

"Yea I see they gave me co-Ed basketball gym I hate that shit," Kim said.

"Why?" Tanya asked.

"I just hate the boys in this school they are idiots. They say all type of dumb shit in the hallway. How you think they gone act in gym when we change into our gym shorts? *Oooh look at that booty, Oooh she got big boobs,*" Kim joked.

Tanya burst out laughing. "It's true, I hate it. Well Kim, if they gonna be watching we better make sure we some fly bitches in our gym gear."

"True, true I'm gonna ask my Dad if he can take us to Macy's to buy us some stuff."

Tanya's face lit up.

**

"Hola mama como esta?" Kim said.

"Hola muñeca ta bien. Como Estés escula??"

"Ta bien mama."

Kim's mother never really spoke English, even though she knew how to. She always spoke to her children in Spanish; she made sure they spoke a second language. Kim never told people she spoke Spanish. She would just play dumb like she didn't understand when she heard others speak, just to see if they talking about her.

When she walked in the living room her dad, brothers and little sister was all watching television.

"But Dad it's gonna be the biggest party of the year" Quincy said.

"Boy please, the year is almost over. We're in September. I don't like that block. Every time it's a party it's a shootout," Luke said.

"Dad nobody messing with me they know I'm not the one." Luke looked at Quincy. Quincy changed his words. Luke gave a sigh, "I will think about it. Who's going with you?"

"Everybody from around here," Quincy quickly responded.

"I wanna go Daddy!" Kim said.

Quincy looked at Kim like she had lost my mind.

"Please Daddy please"

"Kim I don't want you in those types of parties with them hood ass niggas," Luke was serious.

"Dad like Quincy said, all of our friends are gonna be there."

"Kim your friends are not too bright," Luke said quickly.

Quincy and Henry burst out laughing, "Especially Janay she is an air head," said Henry.

"Shut up Henry!" Kim screamed. She turned to her father and then spoke, "Daddy please!"

"Kim I said no."

Kim started to put on her sad puppy face. She knew that this face got her anything she wanted. "Don't start with that look Kim it's not working." Kim's eyes started to tear up. Luke looked at Kim and in his head he said *shit she got me,* but then he thought of something better.

"Kim don't do that. I tell you what; instead of you going to the party I will take you on a shopping spree. You're gonna have twenty five minutes to get everything you want out the store so you better move fast." Kim's face lit up. Quincy's and Henry's mouths dropped. Henry said "that's not fair Dad."

"Stop hating Henry. Ok Daddy can Tanya come with me?" Kim asked.

"Yea she can that's the only friend I like. She's well-mannered and quiet."

In Kim's head she thought, *yea ok Dad that's what you think.*
**

"Ok Kim like I said twenty five minutes," Luke said. Kim and Tanya already came up with a plan. Tanya would go hit up the Guess section and the La Cote Sportif store. Kim decided to hit up the Levi's and sneaker section plus she wanted this MCM book bag for school.

"You ready Kim?" Luke asked.

"Yea Dad I'm ready."

"Alright Go!!!"

Kim and Tanya took off in different directions. Tanya racked up in Guess, picking up two or three things for her then she hit La Cote. Kim killed the Levi section picking up two pairs of reeboks, a pair of Adidas and the newest Jordan's.

"Five more minutes Kim!" Luke yelled.

Shit, Kim thought *my fucking bag,* she ran to the MCM section. "Miss, can I please get the brown and black MCM backpack." The young lady looked at Kim with an attitude. "What you said?" the girl asked Kim. "I said I need the brown and black MCM backpack please." Kim was getting tight she was pressed for time. The girl said "Why? You can't afford that!"

"Excuse me," Kim said, "Bitch how you know what I can and can't afford? Bitch you know me?" The girl face turned red, "Who are you calling a bitch?"

"YOU!!!" Kim yelled. Luke heard Kim from across the room and came running. "What happened Kim?" he asked. "This dumb bitch gonna say I can't afford this MCM book bag. Who she talking to?" Luke already knew once Kim gets mad, it's no stopping her. "Relax Kim," he said.

At this time Tanya came over and spoke, "What this bitch did Kim?" she asked. Kim explained the situation to Tanya and she flipped. "Bitch don't try and play my best friend you mad because you can't afford it?" Luke screamed, "Enough!!" The girl looked scared, knowing she fucked with the wrong one. The girl's manager came by and asked what the problem was. Before the girl could even speak Tanya said, "I'll tell you what's wrong. This bitch doesn't know her place and she needs to be fired." The girl said "bitch shut the fuck up."

Luke was tired of the bullshit. "Listen… listen let me pay for my things and just to show you miss," he paused, "sorry what's your name?" he asked the girl. The girl with an attitude said "Stephanie, why?" Kim said "bitch I will fuck you up talking to my father like that!"
"Kim relax people like Miss Stephanie here you kill with kindness. Stephanie right?" Luke said.
"Yea," she said.
"Give me two MCM backpacks now in two different colors for my baby girl."

Kim was excited, *man fuck that party I'm good now,* she thought. Stephanie rolled her eyes and got the bags. With the two bags, all the clothes and sneakers, Stephanie said "your total is $2,300."

Without hesitation Luke pulled out the biggest stack of hundreds. Stephanie's eyes grew wide. Luke counted out twenty three one hundred dollar bills and told Stephanie to hurry up and bag the stuff. The manager apologized several times. Luke told the gentlemen that his current cashier is bad for business. The manager said, "You're right Sir." He then turned to Stephanie and said, "After you finish helping these customers turn in your name tag. You're fired!!!"

"But But Mr. Smith, I need this job you know I have a son," she cried. Kim and Tanya were laughing. "Well you should have thought about that before you violated," Kim said.

Stephanie looked at Kim and said "don't worry bitch I'm gonna get you."

"I'm right here come and get me" Kim said.

"Enough Kim! Let's go" Luke said.

After leaving the store Luke realized how much he had spent. "2,300 fucking dollars Kim in 25 minutes? Shit. Next time I'm gonna give you five minutes." Luke was upset about the money but he didn't care because he knew he was gonna make that back before the night was done.

Best Friend

"Hi Ma," Tanya said as she walked in the house. "Good Afternoon Tanya" her mother said with her deep Jamaican accent, "Where were you?" she asked.

"I was with Kim and Mr. Luke in Macy's, Kim brought me some sneakers and an outfit for gym class."

"Mi nah like wen dem people give you tings!"

"Ma chill, that's my best friend she always look out for me."

"Mi don't want you fi beg Fren."

Tanya looked at her mother like she was crazy "Ma is you serious? I don't have to do that, not with Kim she's been my friend since we came from Jamaica, relax Ma." Tanya's mother looked at her and rolled her eyes. "Well alright go and bathe your skin so you can eat."

"What's for dinner?" Tanya asked.

"Mi mek stew beef with rice," Tanya's favorite dish.

"Ok Mummi."

Tanya went in her room and sat on her bed. She wished her mother had money like Kim's dad. Tanya's mom came from Jamaica after Tanya's dad got killed in a robbery. Tanya's mother couldn't take it anymore. When Tanya's mother cousin called from the states and invited her to come live with her she packed Tanya up and left.

Tanya thought, *watch one day I'm gonna make enough money to take care of my moms.*

"Tanya!"

"Yes Mummi"

"Pick up de phone. Latrell da pon it."

"Hello" Tanya answered.

"What's up Shorty?"

Tanya smiled; she loved when he called her that.

"Hey La, what you doing?"

"Nothing on the block grinding, how was school?"

"It was ok. Why you didn't come?"

Latrell stayed quiet on the phone.

"Hellooo" Tanya said.

"I hear you Shorty. Man, if I go to school I can't make the money I need to make. You know my pops be beasting wanting me in by a certain time."

"Yea Babe I know, but us getting our diploma is important remember we discussed that so we can get our own."

"Yea but me getting this money so we can have our own is great. Soon we won't have to worry about shit..."

"Ayo L," someone screams in the back.

"Babe I gotta go! Beep me if you need me," La said quickly.

"Okay Latrell." Tanya felt disappointed in him because she knew he would never finish school. Latrell's mind was on money and becoming the next big hustler in Flatbush. He wasn't gonna stop until he made it.

LATRELL

"AYO L," someone screams.

"Babe I gotta go" Latrell hung up the phone as he thought about what Tanya was saying about school and their future. "Man right now I don't have time to think about that, there's money to make," Latrell said to himself.

"YO YO YO what's up Bam?"

Bam was Latrell's best friend. If you saw one the other was not too far behind.

They both had the same goals, to make money and become the next big hustler. Bam was down with the grinding but his thing was robbing. He was the best at it too. Niggas knew what he was about, when Bam came around niggas was on point. "Ain't Shit" Bam said, "just came back from doing this juks I came off with five stacks son and check this out."

When Bam opened his book bag he had three pounds of weed and two packages of coke. Latrell's face lit up. "What the fuck? This is a lot of stuff," L said. Bam was excited "I know now we can come up like we want to, niggas ain't even on selling coke like that. We will be the little niggas out here getting big money." L's mind was racing thinking about so much shit he could do. Bam called his name out.

"Latrell… you down or what??"

 Without hesitation, L screamed out "HELLLLL YEAHHH LET'S GET THIS MONEY!" Bam laughed.

"I'm gonna get my uncle from the Stuy to help us bag up the coke. We still gonna do nickels and tre bags with the weed, agreed?" Bam asked.

"Agreed," L said.

"Now let the hustle begin," Bam said.

Bam gave Latrell $1,500 and said "this for you. Go take care of your fam and buy Tanya something nice." Bam always gave Latrell a cut when he came up on a juks. They were more like brothers than friends. Latrell walked off so hype. He couldn't wait to tell Tanya. Just then he realized the time, "oh shit I'm gonna be late! My pops gonna flip," Latrell started running home, still hype saying to himself tomorrow is a new day and new beginnings.

Change Gonna Come

"Yo I hate going to gym, these boys in this school get on my nerve. They rude as fuck! Especially the ones from our block," Tanya said.

"Well they don't fuck with me," Kim said quickly before she continued, "Because they know Quincy will knock them out."

"That's the truth," Tanya said, "let's just go and get it over with."

When they walked in they noticed they had a new boy in their class. Kim was amazed by his looks. "Oh my god! Tanya do you see the new boy, he so cute!"

"Yea I see," Tanya said.

Both of them were at a standstill just admiring his looks.

There were a lot of whispers from the others girls. Everybody wanted to know his name. "Alright alright settle down class," said Mr. Butler. "We have a new student his is Tyreek Smith. He's gonna be starting on our basketball team. I expect everyone to be nice to him." *Oh I will be nice to him alright,* Kim thought. After class everybody was introducing themselves to him.

"Let's go Tanya,"

"Kim you don't wanna meet him?" Tanya asked.

Tanya grabbed Kim's arm. "Damn, y'all act like he's Puff Daddy or something. I will see him around," Kim said as she turned to walk out. Tyreek watched as Kim and Tanya walked out of the gym without saying anything to him. He was impressed by Kim looks and her whole attitude.

**

Kim walked to her other class thinking about Tyreek. "Kim? Hellloo Kim?" Kim snapped out of her thoughts when she heard Tanya calling her name.

"Huh?"

"Girl what's wrong with you?"

"Oh nothing, just thinking."

Kim regretted not talking to Tyreek but she knew that there would be another time.

After school Tanya and Kim walked to McDonald's to get something to eat. McDonald's was the hang out spot, kids used to sit in there every day. They would cut class or meet up after school before they went home. When they got in McDonald's to their surprise Latrell, Bam and some other dudes was sitting in there. Tanya's face lit up when she saw La. She hadn't seen him in a couple of days. "Yo La! Look who just walked in" Bam said.

Latrell turned around and saw Tanya. Inside he was hype to see her but around his mans he fronted like it wasn't nothing.

"Hey guys" Kim said.

"What's up Kim" everybody said.

"Kim when you gonna stop acting stuck up and give me a chance?" Kim looked at Bam and laughed,

"Are you serious? Aren't you with Kisha Scott?"

"NO, we been broke up she was fronting on them draws" Bam said as he and all his friends started to laugh.

Kim didn't think it was funny. She rolled her eyes and walked away. "So what's up La? Why haven't I heard from?" Tanya asked. Latrell looked at her and said "I been busy making money." He gave Bam a pound, feeling hype that they were finally seeing money. Tanya looked at him with anger. "So just because you're making money you can't call me or come see me."

Latrell started to feel annoyed so he snapped at her "NO! Get off my back, damn!" Everybody in McDonald's turned around and looked at Tanya. Tanya was in shock, with tears in her eyes as she ran out of the door. "Damn La, you didn't have to do that to her. That girl love your ugly ass" Bam laughed then continued, "go get her."

"Nah yo, I don't have time for that. Yo what's up with our next move? The weed is moving fast and everybody getting hooked on this coke. We need to get more supply."

"Chill La, I have a plan in action. I'm staking out these Jamaicans up on Linden. If things go good we will be sitting lovely."

La was excited but felt bad at the same time about what he just did to Tanya. "Damn I hate McDonald's! The line is always long." Kim said. She looked around for her friend. "Yo where is Tanya?" she asked. Everybody looked at La.

"What did you do Latrell?" Kim asked.

"Nothing! She was just asking me mad questions, she got mad and left."

Kim shook her head. "Why you have to be an asshole sometimes La? Let me go look for Tee." Kim started to walk out the door.

"Kim wait" Latrell said.

"What!" Kim yelled.

"Yo please tell her I'm sorry and I'm gonna make it up to her." he said.

"Latrell, Tanya always had your back and you shit on her all the time," Kim said.

"Just please tell her that Kim damn."

Kim walked away and said "whatever."

As Kim was walking down Church Avenue she noticed a familiar face. It was Tyreek. Kim smiled and thought to herself, *DAMN he looks good,* thinking if she should she say something to him or not. Just as she was about to walk across the street a girl walked up and hugged him. Kim eyes opened wide, *this Bitch.* Kim realized the girl he was hugging was the girl from Macy's awhile back that she had an argument with. Tyreek picked her son up and gave him a kiss. Stephanie and Tyreek started walking off. Kim just stood there looking confused. Kim thought, *yo I can end that real quick. I must go tell Tanya.* Kim walked off in a hurry hoping she caught Tanya before she went in the house.

Just To Get a Rep

Bam sat in his Saab automobile with his two homeboys from Bedstuy, ShaKim and Mel. They were all staking out the weed spot on Linden Boulevard. They had been out there for three hours. He knew they was gonna be out there for a minute so he made sure that they had food, drinks and smokes. "Yea Shorty was all over me at the party, she was dope." ShaKim said.

Mel said "she's alright... Why you sweating her?"

"Nigga you mad cause you was rapping to her and she dissed you."

ShaKim laughed, "Whatever I wasn't feeling her anyway."

Bam just listened to them talk. He was too busy watching the house, seeing who comes in and out. "Yoooo this my shit turn the radio up," Mel said. Gang Starr was on the radio:

Stick up kid is out to tax.
Brother are amused by other brother's rep but the thing they
know best is where the gun is kept.
cause in the night, you'll feel fright
and at the sight of a 4-5th, I guess you just might

want to do a dance or two
cause they could maybe bust you for self or wit a crew.
no matter is you or your brother's a star he could pop you in
check without a getaway car.
and some might say he's a dummy
but he sticking you and taking all of your money,
just to get a rep...

"Yo, I'm not gonna lie this my shit too," Bam said. He was nodding to the beat but he still paid attention on his target. Just when he thought the coast was clear he gave out his instruction. "Sha I need you on the side of the house. Mel you hit the back. I will go through the front. My mans said they keep everything in the living room in the fireplace. Y'all just have my back. If things go as planned, this will change all our lives for good."

ShaKim and Mel nodded their heads agreeing with Bam. All of them put their mask on and checked their guns. "LET'S ROLL" Bam whispered. As they approached the house they noticed all the lights were off except the light from the television. Bam motioned for ShaKim to go to the side of the house, Mel was already in position. All Mel kept thinking was, *I'm gonna get this money and blow up.* Bam took his tool out and popped the lock. He walked in the front door as quiet as can be.

When he approached the living room, one nigga was laying on the couch while a bitch was sucking his dick. "Lawd God! Mi nah no how you do it my gyal" the dude said. The girl lifted her head and said "you like that?" Bam's eyes opened wide as he whispered "this bitch Kisha." Bam got tight knowing this bitch fronted on him and told him she was a virgin. The dude took Kisha and flipped her around and then started fucking her. Kisha was screaming and moaning so loud that, the dude didn't even hear Bam come in the living room. He didn't hear the back door open either.

Mel came in quick and made eye contact with Bam. "Fuck me! Yes!" Kisha screamed. "You want da cocky my gyal" the dude said. Bam couldn't bear anymore. "I tell you what I want nigga," Bam yelled. The dude turned around and Bam gun butted him.

"A what di bumba clot a you do."

"Shut the fuck up," Mel said, "where the money at Homie."

"Mi nah have no money bedren."

Kisha started screaming. "Shut up bitch!" Bam said as he slapped her. Kisha fell on the floor. Bam was livid that she played him. "Listen I don't have time for games just give us the stash and the drugs and we out," he said.

"My youth mi done tell ya mi nah have nuttin"

"Jarret, please give them the stuff," Kisha cried.

"My gyal don't call my name" Jarret said. Bam went straight to the fireplace and pulled the laundry bag out. "JACK POT," he said once he felt the bag in his hand.

Bam opened the bag and it was filled with cash, another bag came falling out the fireplace followed by another one. Bam had all that he came for. He was so amazed that he didn't even see Jarret reach for his gun. Two shots let off. Jarret shot Mel in the head. Mel dropped to the floor. Jarret turned the gun on Bam but the gun jammed. ShaKim came in and put four bullets in Jarret. Bam thought he was a dead man. Kisha wouldn't stop screaming. Sha said "shut up bitch" and punched Kisha in her face. "Chill son!" Bam said. He was mad at her but he didn't want to see her get beat up. "What we doing with this bitch?" Sha said. Bam looked at her for a long time. He thought about taking the pussy but he thought of what he saw when he walked in.

He just looked at Sha and said "finish her." He walked out and Sha gave her two shots to the head. Bam and ShaKim ran to the car and sped off. When they got back to the Stuy they sat in silence for a while in the car. They both had tears in their eyes thinking about how they just lost Mel. Sha said "what I'm gonna tell his moms and his girl, she pregnant."

Bam just sat in silence. "We still gonna split these two bags three ways. Sha you gonna give his mom and baby his part. Split down the middle between the both of them. Look let's go upstairs and do what we have to do. Stay low key for a while." Bam's mind was on the extra bag he had and his plans of heading O.T. *I have to go see La,* he thought.

Sacrifice

"TANYA, TANYA WAIT UP" Kim yelled. Tanya was in another world, the drama that she and Latrell had been going through had her down and depressed. She hadn't been to school and hadn't been answering Kim's calls. Kim grabbed her hand, Tanya got scared. "Hey what's up, I been calling for two days." Kim said. "I just was in my own world. I was sick," Tanya responded. Kim knew her best friend was lying. "Tanya you can't make Latrell have you like this you have to snap out of it."

"I have been with him for so long. He's my first love and the only one I ever had sex with," she paused, "Why is he treating me like this?"

"Cause he's an idiot. He's into the streets Tee. He thinks he's the man because he's making money," Kim said.

"I called his house and his dad said he doesn't live there anymore."

"WHAT!!" Kim was in shock, "so where does he live?"

"Kim I don't know. Let's walk around his way and see if we see him."

Tanya and Kim started walking down Flatbush. "BITCH!! I knew I had to tell you something. So why the day we were in

McDonald's I was walking to check on you and guess who the fuck I saw?"

"Who?" Tanya asked.

"Tyreek. But guess who he was with?" Tanya looked at Kim in suspense.

"Who bitch?"

"Stephanie!"

"Who's that?" Tanya asked in a confused state.

"The chick, the girl from Macys we was gonna fuck up," Kim said in an excited manner.

"Ooooooohh wow!! How he know her?" Tanya asked.

"I don't know" Kim said, "he was with her and he was holding a baby."

"A BABY!!" Tanya screamed.

"Yes Girl!"

"But he's too young to have a baby," Tanya said as she pouted.

"I know right but I don't know, they looked like a family."
**

As they walked up Tilden they noticed Bam and Latrell on the corner with a group of people. When they got closer, Tanya's eyes opened wide when she saw Latrell hugged up with another bitch. Kim looked at Tanya and saw her face. She had to think quickly, "Tanya let's go, fuck him. Let's just go!" Tanya started to cry and get upset. "NO! FUCK THAT." Tanya started walking fast, "Tanya wait!" Kim yelled. Latrell didn't even see Tanya coming. Bam turned around when he saw Tanya coming but it was too late to tell La. Tanya snuffed Latrell in the face "WHAT THE FUCK YOU DOING LA?" she screamed as she threw blows. Latrell's face was shocked, in his head he was saying, *fuck fuck what the hell I'm gonna say.*

"Bitch don't put your hands on my man!!" The girl standing beside La said. Tanya and Kim looked at each other, turned to Latrell and at the same time said "MAN??" Latrell just stood there still in shock, he didn't say a word. "YES Bitches! Marquis is my man!" the young lady said with a little accent. "WHO THE FUCK YOU CALLING A BITCH? LATRELL LET THIS BITCH KNOW WE ARE NOT THE ONE TO PLAY WITH!! BITCH WHO THE FUCK IS YOU?" Kim screamed.
"My name is Marsha and WE live together in Rochester," the girl said as she pointed to herself and Latrell.

Tanya just looked at Latrell but he still wasn't saying anything. "How could you do this to me La?" Tanya asked as she cried, "after all we been through. I love you! Why the fuck is she calling you Marquise?" Tanya started pushing Latrell but he still was not saying anything. Bam was standing there looking amused by the excitement until he heard Marsha say that they lived in Rochester together. He thought, *damn all our hard work about to be fucked up. We finally up; we took over a town and shorty helping us. Nah I have to stop this.* "Oh LA! What the fuck! Why you not saying nothing?" Tanya yelled at a vacant Latrell.

"Yo Tee chill, let me talk to him," Bam said.

"Bam how can he do this to me? Tanya cried.

"Tee let me see what's going on please stop crying sis. Just hold on" Bam pleaded with her.

Bam loved Tanya like she was his real sister but he didn't love her more than money.

"YO! My nigga you better put this shit to an end." Bam said.

"Bam I fucked up, I fucked up," Latrell was holding his head, "what the fuck I'm gonna do Bam? WHAT!!"

"What the fuck you mean?" Bam asked.

"Bro I can't lose Tanya. I love her," Latrell's heart was breaking.

"Yo my nigga, if you diss Marsha it's a wrap for us in Chester. We finally making the money we always wanted. Nigga we run that town. You have to sacrifice some things bro, even if it's losing Tanya. When we come back you can move her out her mom's crib and have your own house with her, that's how much bread you will have."

Latrell thought for a second, he put his head down and said "DAMN!" Latrell walked to Tanya and said "look Ma, me and you haven't been right in a minute, I mean I'm doing bigger things now. Things you're not ready for, you feel me?" Tanya looked at him in shock with tears in her eyes. Kim looked at her friend and saw her heartbreaking. That shit made her fucking tight. "Latrell you're whack! Tanya was always there for your dumb ass, you pussy for that!" Latrell looked at Kim, "YO! On some real shit Kim mind your fucking business, you lucky I have respect for your brothers or else I would have slapped the shit out of you."

Hearing him say that Kim broke fool, "nigga you know I'm not pussy and I have no fucking problem fighting your punk ass." Marsha screamed out "Bitch! Don't talk to my man like that! I will fuck your bum ass up." Without thinking Kim grabbed shorty by the hair and gave her the business. "Bitch I told you we are not the one!" Kim yelled as she body slammed Marsha on the floor and then dragged her up and down Tilden. Latrell tried to break it up but Tanya wasn't having that. "Don't touch my fucking friend or else I will slice this bitch up." Latrell just stopped and looked at Tanya.

"I'm sorry Tanya!" he mumbled.

"Fuck you Latrell!" Tanya screamed.

Kim was stomping shorty out. Marsha was screaming "Marquise get her off of me!"

Bam grabbed Kim, "chill Kim you trying to kill her?" "Bam let this bitch know, don't come to my town and pop shit she will get it every time. Tanya let's go! Fuck him!" Kim took Tanya and walked away. Once they got a block away Tanya stopped and let out a big scream. Kim got scared. "How can he do this to me after all we've been through?" Kim just let her friend get all of her emotions out. She was so mad at Latrell and thought, *I will step to him one on one when I see him.*

**

Latrell sat on the block drinking a bottle of Remy. Thinking to himself that he messed up his shot with his one true love. Bam walked over to La and said "Look, it doesn't make any sense for you to think about shit. It's done bro. What you need to be doing is making sure Shorty good. Remember without her, we can't make any moves out there. After we get the package we out, oh and by the way, my cousin Nu-black coming with us."

"Bam you know that nigga 7/30 he might fuck shit up," La said.

"Relax I got him" Bam said, "You just worry about the money."

Out with Old, In With New

A couple of months had gone by, Thanksgiving, Christmas even the New Year had passed. Things were going good in the Shepherd's home. Luke's number spot was doing great, the boys were still on their getting money shit, and Maria was still taking care of their home and her youngest daughter. Kim had begun to go on missions with the girls except Tanya. Ever since she and Latrell broke up she had been distant. She wasn't coming to school as much; she wasn't answering phone calls, nothing. She had seen Latrell in passing but they never spoke.

Latrell was doing very well for himself. He and Bam were the main drug dealers in their hood, everybody was on their dick. They were still going in and out of town. Their crew had begun to grow. Latrell and Bam just brought themselves new cars. Both of them were driving the Cressidas that just came out. Bam gave his old Saab to his cousin Nu-black.

All three were making money and living life. Even though Nu-black was just a runner, he dreamt about doing his own shit. His dreams was getting his own connect someday. He just knew he would have to do some grimy shit. Latrell sat on the block thinking how his life had changed a lot.

Even though he didn't really fuck with his father like that he always went and checked on him. All his pops cared about was the money Latrell was giving him. Tanya was always on his mind. He passed her house every time he came back to Brooklyn. He always wanted to go talk to her but he never had the heart to face her. But he thought today would be a good day to try to speak to her. "Yo Bam I'll be back. I'm gonna make a run real quick" Latrell jumped in his car and went straight to Tanya's house.

Latrell buzzed the bell three times. He waited for a while, there was no answer. In his mind he thought *where could she be?* He buzzed the bell one more time "Who is it?" he heard. His heart started racing, "its Latrell, Tee"

"What do you want?" Tanya asked.

"Please can I talk to you? I need to talk to you."

Tanya stood looking at the intercom for a second. Thinking *what should I do?* Finally she buzzed him upstairs.

Latrell ran up to the third floor. This was the only chance he had to explain and say sorry. When he got to the door she was standing there with her arms folded. His heart was racing.

"What do you want Latrell?" Tanya said.

"What's up Tee? How are you?"

"Why do you care how I'm doing?"

"Come on Tee, I'm gonna always care," he said.

Tanya looked at him with tears in her eyes and said "OH REALLY!! You didn't care when you was in front of your bitch!"

"Look, Shorty only around to help move this work. She helps us," La said quickly.

"She helps y'all? Or she helps you by fucking you?"

Latrell put his head down, "look that just happened I don't love her, I love you Tee, and I'm doing this for us Tee. This is all we ever talked about." Tanya started crying, "You played me Latrell. You made me look like a fool in front of my friends and your friends." Latrell grabbed her and started hugging her. "I'm sorry Shorty. Please forgive me, please," Latrell went in his pocket and pulled out a stack of money. Here Tee this is two stacks go shopping Baby. Buy you and your mother something. See Babe, you don't have to worry about Kim getting you shit, I got us."

Tanya's heart started to melt, she was so in love with La but she couldn't get over the fact that he was living out of town with another bitch. Tanya looked up at Latrell with tears in her eyes. "Do you love me Latrell?" she asked. Latrell grabbed her face and kissed her on her lips "of course I do Tanya, I will always love you," he answered honestly. That's all Tanya wanted to hear. "So it wouldn't be hard for you to choose. Come back home and leave the drug game alone," she said excitedly. Latrell stepped back and looked at Tanya and said "and do what Tee? Go back to school? Live back with my father? Be broke? Live off of dreams?"

"Get a job La, you can take night classes. My mom works five days out of the week now so she's only home on the weekend. You can stay with me."

Damn I love this girl, Latrell thought and he wanted so much with her, kids, marriage and all. But he wasn't ready to give up the game that easy, not when he was on top. "Tanya I love you so much but Baby I'm sorry I can't do that," he said. Tanya's heart broke in two. "Then I guess this is it. Here take your money back Latrell."

"No Tee that's for you, please understand that I'm doing this for us. You may not think so now, but you will," Latrell said with tears in his eyes. "Goodbye Latrell I wish you well," Tanya said in-between sobs. "Tanya please don't do this," he begged

Tanya closed her door and Latrell just stood there in silence. On the other side of the door Tanya cried her heart out and he heard it. The one she truly loved was no longer hers. Latrell drove back to the hotel. As soon as he got in the door Marsha asked "where the hell you been? I was paging you!" "Taking care of business and don't ask me no fucking questions!!" he shouted. Marsha was in shock. Latrell went and took a hot shower and then lay on the bed. His thought was all over the place. The radio was on WBLS and Lose Control came on by Silk. *DAMN! This is Tanya's song,* he thought as he closed his eyes and just listened to the words.

Last night we had an argument
You told me you love me
All the things I said I never meant
No baby
I didn't mean to make you cry
I didn't mean to make you say bye bye bye
Baby won't you let me look inside your soul
Let me make you lose control
Let me be the one you need
Baby just come to me
Now tell me girl what you want from me
Whatever it is you desire
I want to give my baby
I want to feel your body yearn
All your softest spots I plan to learn
Baby won't you let me just kiss you down
Make you spin around and 'round
Flip you girl from left to right

If you don't mind
Baby can I just spend the night....

His thoughts were interrupted when he heard Marsha ask "Babe, are you okay?"

"Yes just tired," La said.

"Well here, I rolled you a spliff and poured you a drink," she said.

La started sipping and smoking. He started to feel real nice. Marsha began kissing on his neck and his chest, and then began sucking on his dick. Latrell felt like he was on cloud nine.

"Baby you like that?" Marsha asked.

"You know I do," La whispered. Marsha continued. Latrell loved Tanya but he had to do what he had to do. Latrell looked at Marsha with lust in his eyes and said "Babe, let's go home."

Yo Shorty!!

Kim and her girls were walking down Flatbush one night on their way to the Afrika House Club. There was a popping party that night; Eternity Sounds was playing the music. Tanya said "we have to hurry y'all; you know it's free before eleven and five dollars after and half of y'all bitches don't have two dollars."

"Alright we coming" Janay screamed. Kim turned to Tanya, "I'm glad you're coming back around I really missed you."

"I missed you too Kim! After Latrell came to visit me and he made his decision I thought I was gonna die. But I had to learn to try and move on. The money he gave me I put up for a rainy day. Now that I'm working at Burger King and taking night classes I don't have time to think about him."

"Yea, you're right" Kim said.

**

"Yo Hassan what's good" Kim's friend Mary said.

Hassan looked across the street "what's up Mary, where y'all headed to?"

"Afrika House" Mary yelled.

"Oh Okay!"

Kim looked across the street and her and Hassan's eyes met. Hassan was dark skinned and well built. Hassan smiled and all you saw was some pretty white teeth. Kim was amazed by his smile, she smiled and then turned away, feeling shy, her heart started racing.

"Yo Mary who is that?" Kim asked.

"Oh that's Hassan he's from Ave C side."

"Damn he looks good," Kim said.

Mary laughed and then turned around and said, "Yo Hassan my friend said you look good..."

"MARY!" Kim yelled feeling embarrassed, but happy at the same time. Hassan said "so, what's up?"

"Mary don't call him over here please," Kim pleaded.

"Why you acting like that girl? Stop being scared all the time to talk to somebody. You always thinking Quincy gonna beat up everybody you talk to." Mary stated.

"LOOK I don't want any problems," Kim said.

"Don't worry I got you, now let's go party," Mary said.

**

Afrika House was jumping everybody was in there. Tennis Court and East 21st were deep. Eternity Sounds was killing it.

"What up Songui!" Kim said.

"Hey Kim, what's good?" The D.J said.

"I see you rocking out," Kim said.

"Yea I'm trying I hope you enjoy the party Kim."

As soon as Kim walked away from the D.J he got on the mic.

"Shout Out to My Tennis Court Girls in the Building."

The party was rocking Kim and her girls were the center of attention. The D.J shouted again, "Tennis Court Ladies this is for you…"

Ooh OOh Baby, I love you my lady,
I love you sweet baby yeah

Sometimes I wonder
How I'd ever make it through
Through this world without having you
I just wouldn't have a clue

'Cause sometimes it seems
Like this world's closing in on me
And there's no way of breaking free
And then I see you reach for me

Sometimes I wanna give up
I wanna give in
I wanna quit the fight
And then I see you, baby
And everything's alright
Everything's alright

When I see you smile
I can face the world, oh oh
You know I can do anything

"This is my song" Kim said. She closed her eyes and started whining real slow, suddenly she felt someone's arms wrap around her waist, when she turn around all she saw was those white teeth. She smiled when she saw that it was Hassan. Her heart was beating a mile a minute, but she was happy. She turned back around and danced with him for three songs. Her body started feeling warm, when she noticed he was catching a hard on she began to get wet.

Just when it was getting real a fight broke out. Mary grabbed Kim's hand and said "Let's Go!" Kim looked at Hassan and he looked back at her. They both didn't say a word. Kim and her friends all ran out of the club. When they got a block away they heard gunshots. "Oh my God I hope nobody we know got hurt" Janay said. "Word" Mary said, "Come on let go to La Cabana and get some food, plus you know everybody goes there after the club you never know who you might bump into," Mary said as she looked at Kim and winked her eye.

Kim smiled and said "Come on Tanya let's go"
"I really wanna go home Kim I'm tired," Tanya said.
"Please, Please Tanya let's just go for a little while. Remember I can't go home, I told my parents that I'm sleeping by you."
Tanya really wanted to leave but she didn't want to play Kim. "Ok Kim just for a little while." Kim was hype, "you never know Tanya you might find somebody new." Tanya just looked at her, "Whatever Kim." They both laughed and ran to catch up with the girls.
**

When they walked into La Cabana it was crazy packed. Everybody was talking about the party. Mary called out "Hey Eddie let me get some chicken and French fries." "Chu got it!" Eddie said. La Cabana was the best Spanish restaurant in Flatbush. Everybody used to hang out there. All the kids after school, church people, and the local crackheads and of course the drug dealers. All drug transactions went down in there. Kim and her girls was laughing and cracking mad jokes. "Somebody was crazy open when she got that dance from Hassan." All the girls looked at Kim then began to laugh. Kim's face turned red, she was feeling embarrassed. "Shut up Mary," Kim said before she started laughing as well. "Oooh girl. I felt like I was on cloud nine. I don't know y'all it's something about him. He's gonna be my baby daddy," Kim said jokingly.

"DAMN, off of one dance?" Mary asked as they all laughed.

Just then Bam walked in with some out of town cats. Kim kicked Tanya under the table to motion for her to turn around. Once she saw Bam she thought La was right behind him, but unfortunately, he wasn't. Tanya felt sad. Truth be told, she was missing Latrell. But since he had moved on, it was time for her to do the same she thought. "Heyyy ladies." Bam shouted.

"Hey Bam," everyone said in unison.

"Is it me or does Bam look good as hell?" Mary asked. Kim looked at her in disbelief. "Bitch it's just you," Kim said.

"So Bam what's going on with you?" Mary asked.

"What Mary I'm chilling just out here making this money."

The sound of money always made Mary hype. Mary was one of those chicks that were about her business, she dabbled in the drug game here and there. Mary loved to gamble. Niggas could not fuck with her in a dice game; she always left with a thousand and better. She was no joke. "Well maybe one day we can go out to eat or something" Bam looked at Mary and thought, *damn I always wanted to fuck her.* With Mary as his shorty he couldn't lose.

He already knew what type of chick she was. He thought while he was O.T she could hold him down. He finished thinking and said "no doubt I'm leaving in two days maybe we can meet up tomorrow. Mary smiled and then said "Okay." Songui came rushing in the door. "Yoooo that fight was crazy!!" he said.

"What up Gui!" Bam said.

"Oh shit Bam what's up."

"Who was fighting?" Bam asked.

"Parkside niggas and Ave C Niggas. They were going crazy. Your boy was there Bam; he got locked for a gun."

Bam's eyes opened up wide, "WHO?" he asked.

"Hassan, that nigga was knocking everybody out. He sliced Mac in the face. Just when he pulled out the gun the police pulled up and jumped on him."

"WORD!!!!" Bam said in disbelief.

Mary and Kim looked at each other. "Well there goes your baby daddy dreams" Mary whispered. Kim felt so sad. Just when she started to like somebody his ass had to get locked up. *Oh well,* she thought, *it was good even if it was only one dance.*

Let's get it on...

Mary was patiently waiting in front of her house for Bam. He was already forty-five minutes late. She quickly called Kim. "Girl I'm still waiting for this dude," she said. "Why you want to go out with him? You never like him before," Kim responded.

"Kim before he was broke now he's making crazy cash. So now he's cute."

They both laughed. "Girl I have to call you back, he's here." Mary hung up the phone so fast and went outside.

"What up Shorty?" Bam said. "How may I help you Bam?" she asked. Bam looked at Mary like he was confused.

"What you mean, how may I help you? I thought we had a date?"

"YEAH, we did but you're like forty-five minutes late. So I'm staying home."

"You serious Ma? I had to run around and collect this bread so we can go out. I had to make sure I have enough money, can't half step on you Shorty I know what type of female you are."

Mary stood and looked at Bam thinking to herself should she go. *That nigga went and got some money for me, I'm gonna spend every bit,* she thought to herself. "I'm gonna let you slide this time." Bam smiled, "we need to stop on the block. I just wanna drop this package off." Mary and Bam went on Tilden to drop the package off. "FUCK!" Bam screamed.

"What's wrong?" Mary asked.

"My ex is in front of the building. I hate that bitch," he said. Mary knew exactly who he was talking about. Sandra was some bitch from Lenox Road. She and Mary had some beef back in the days. When Sandra and her friends jumped Mary. Mary thought, *I can finally get this bitch.* But instead she kept her cool. When Sandra saw Bam and Mary pull up her face turned red. Bam jumped out and ran in the building.

"What Up Mary" Bam's cousin said.

"What up Black." Mary kept her eyes on Sandra just in case she tried anything. Bam came back out the building and stopped, he was speaking to Black.

Sandra walked up to him. "Oh so you can't fucking speak now?" she asked. "For what? Yo get out of my face," Bam said quickly. Sandra was heated. "Oh really now it's get out of your face? Why? Cause you with that bitch?" That's all Mary needed to hear to come out that car. "What happened? You have something to say?" she said. Mary was just waiting for her to speak so she could cut her ass up. Mary was one of those chicks that carried a blade in her mouth. She was ruthless with it.

"No one was talking to you, mind your business bitch," Sandra said. "BITCH! Bam is my business," Mary said.

Bam's eyes widen and he smiled. It felt good to know that Mary was repping him. "Oh Word! Is this true Bam? This your new girl?" Sandra was getting so upset. "What she just told you," Bam screamed, "GET OUT OF HERE!!" Sandra felt embarrassed. She looked at Bam with tears in her eyes, then turned and looked at Mary and thought, *I'm gonna get you bitch.* Sandra quickly walked away. Mary looked at Sandra as she was walking away and already knew this wasn't the last time she was gonna see her. She wasn't worried about her; her mind was on Bam and his money.

Now that she opened her big mouth like she was truly his girl, it was time that she played her part. Bam was still tight that Sandra came around. *The bitch doesn't even live over here,* he thought to himself. Plus he was also upset that his cousin fucked up his money. Just when he was deep in thought Mary called his name. "What you doing staying on the block all day? I thought we had a date?" Bam looked at her and smiled "yea let's get out of here."

Bam knew from then it was gonna be on and popping.

**

Mary and Bam went to Junior's. They got a table, ordered some food and drinks and just sat and talked for hours it seemed like. Mary was tipsy off the Remy. "Let's get out of here." She said. "Where you wanna go?" he asked? Bam hoped she said the hotel. He had been feenin to fuck for a couple of years now. "Anywhere." Mary thought, I *hope this is worth it. If this nigga is wack I'm gonna die.* Bam thought quickly, since he was leaving in the next three hours he kept it local. "Let's go to my Aunt's house, She's not home she works overnight."

Bam pulled up in front of his aunt's house and for some reason he was nervous. He wanted shawty for so long now that he had her, he didn't want to fuck it up. Mary sat in the car thinking should she really go in the house with him. *Shit, I know if I give him this good pussy, he's gonna be open.* Plus she thought she had to do it to put her plan in motion. "You ready shawty?" The sound of Bam's voice made Mary jump. "You alright?" he asked.
"Yea just a little chilly," she said. "Well, let's get inside so I can warm you up," She smiled at him. But in her mind she thought, *I hope I'm not making a mistake.*

When they walked in the house, Mary was shocked at how the house was decorated. "This house is fly" she said. Bam smiled and said thanks. "I make sure my Aunt is good. She's been raising me since I was three. I moved here after my mom died." Mary felt sad. "How did she die?" she asked. "Don't wanna talk about it." Bam snapped! "Let's go in my room," he said. Mary never asked about his mother again.

When she got in the room she was amazed as well. He had all of the latest things. Mary was so open off of the things she saw. She kept a mental note of everything. "Sit Down Boo. Don't tell me you're scared now?" Bam said. "Boy please scared of what?" she responded. But in all actuality she was a little nervous. *I'm gonna need another drink for this performance,* she thought before she spoke.

"You got more Remy?" she asked.

"Hell yea let me get you a cup."

Bam ran to get the cup. He then poured her a drink.

"Here Babe," he said as he handed her the cup.

"Thank you."

Mary began to drink her Remy, she started feeling warm. "It's hot in here." She said as she took her shirt off. Bam's dick began to get hard. "Damn you have a sexy body." he said. He started to rub her breast. He unsnapped her bra and began to suck on her nipples. Mary began to moan, she took another sip of the Remy. Now at this time she was drunk. Bam put his hands down her pants and started playing with her. "Damn you're wet. Yo, I got to get in this pussy now." He whispered. He started taking his clothes off then he took her clothes off. He climbed on top and began to kiss her all over.

He started putting his fingers inside of her. Mary began to go crazy. "Fuck me Bam!" she said. That's all he wanted to hear. Bam slid inside her. "Wait Wait" Mary yelled, "Where is your condom?"

"Babe we don't need that" Bam said.

"Oh yes we do, I don't know who you fucking Bam. You got Sandra coming on your block. I don't fuck with that bitch!"

"Babe it's me and you now. You my girl, I been wanted you. You think I want to lose you?" he asked sweetly.

Mary started blushing. "Put some music on." she said.

Bam jumped off the bed to turn on the radio, he was searching the station. When he stopped at 98.7 kiss F.M the perfect song was on....

Every time I close my eyes
I wake up feeling so horny
I can't get you outta my mind
Sexin' you be all I see

I would give anything
Just to make you understand me
I don't give damn about nothing else
Freek'n you is all I need.

"I love me some Jodeci" Mary whispered. Bam began to kiss on her neck again, this time leaving hickeys all over her. Mary was so into feeling the buzz from the Remy, she didn't realize that Bam never put on the condom. Bam entered Mary and he felt like he was in heaven. "DAMNNNN why is it soooo warm inside?" Bam asked. Mary moaned louder. To her surprise Bam's dick game was off the hook. She thought that she could get used to this. Bam started pumping her faster and harder. Mary's body started to shake. "OH MY GOD I'M COMING!" she screamed. "Me too Baby," Bam yelled. They both made a loud moan and then collapsed on the bed. They both were hot and sweating. Bam turned to Mary, kissed her on the forehead and said "I want you to be my girl."

Mary was quiet for a minute. "Babe you hear me?" he asked.
"I hear you Bam."
"So why you so quiet?" he asked.

Mary thought long and hard before she answered. "I don't want any drama you got going on with these other bitches."

"Bitches? What other bitches?" Bam knew she was talking about Sandra, "I don't have any other Bitches!" Mary looked at him with a screwed face. "NIGGA PLEASE! So what was that earlier with Sandra? Don't tell me she's just a crazy chick."

Bam laughed "Nah, I used to fuck with her a while back she did some grimy shit so I cut her off. She mad because I don't want her back. I haven't been fucking anybody. I been too busy going O.T."

"So what makes you think you're gonna have time for me now Bam?"

"Cause your gonna come with me out of town. I know with you as my girl, we can kill it. Even if I'm not home I know you would hold us down. We can make all this money."

Mary smiled, "Ok Bam I'll be your girl, but I wanna be spoiled. I want these bitches to be jealous because my boyfriend gets me everything I want." Bam laughed "I got you Ma. Tomorrow we can go shopping. We will hit up Kings Plaza and get you some things. Now, can I get some more pussy? That shit so good."

Mary looked at him with a smirk on her face. *I have to play my part if I want my plan to work,* she thought. She looked at Bam and said, "Come get it...."

On To Da Next...

Months had passed. Kim had been so busy with this job that her Dean got her. She registered for a program so that she could graduate out of school early. She was at her last few months in the program. Kim hadn't seen Tanya in a while. They both had been working and ever since the breakup with Latrell, Tanya had been distant. She was staying with her cousins in Brownsville. She started dating some dude from Seth Low Projects, now from what the streets were saying about Ray, he was a hot head and he was always in some shit. Ray was a stickup kid. That nigga was running around robbing any and everything. If he heard you got it, he's coming for it. Friends only stayed around him because they didn't want to be a victim. Ray had all the latest shit; he was riding around in the New Eddie Bauer Truck. He was one of the first niggahs in his hood with it. Bitches stayed around him and his crew. They knew they were about that money.

Tanya met Ray at her cousin's party in Albany Manor. Her cousin invited everybody from Brownsville to Flatbush, the club was jam packed. Tanya and her cousin wore cut up tights, bodysuits and the latest travel fox sneakers. Everybody was sweating them. Her hair was done by the hottest beautician in Flatbush, Suzette from Shear Perfection. They rocked their door knockers, Gucci links and bangles. The hottest Djs was on the set, Eternity Sounds, Mustang International, and Mega Tone. The music was rocking. Tanya and her cousins were having a blast. Smoking their spliffs and popping bottles of Canei. Tanya was in the middle of the dance floor whining her waist to the reggae music.

"NOW TANYA!!" The DJ shouted out, "Next Tune for You."

All of a sudden Lady Saw's voice came through the speaker…

if him lef and nuh my pussy fault
di only fault mi pussy hav a fi chipp di hood rass
mi posess wid di good underneath
wen mi man a fuck di pussy him nuh stop skin him teeth
he say it tight eeeeee
seh mi cyaant get in, look pon di dresser
pass mi di vaseline
Oil it down nuh
yuh kno mi nah dream, you are 22 and yuh feel like 13
gyal skin out, mek mi try mi finger first coz wuyy yuh pussy
tight like a tight tus
if him lef an nuh my pussy fault di only fault di pussy have a fi
chipp di hood rass

Me possess with the good underneath
when mi man ah fuck the pussy, watch dis

Tanya was caught up in the music. "YESS AH MI CUZZIN DAT!!!" Tanya's cousin, Patsy, yelled. As Tanya kept dancing and having a ball, she looked over to her left and there he was clocking her down. Tanya stopped dancing and looked at him for a minute. "Damn, he looks good" Tanya mumbled to herself. Ray and Tanya were staring at each other for a few minutes until some dude tried to dance with Tanya. He grabbed her from behind and started whining on her ass slow.

Tanya turned around and pushed the guy off and said, "YO what the fuck you doing?"

"Damn Shawty I can't dub on that fat ass?" The dude asked all drunk grabbing on Tanya hand.

"GET THE FUCK OFF OF ME!!" she yelled.

"Or else what?"

Just then Ray pushed the dude and said "Or else it's gonna be a real problem. Get your hand off my girl." The dude looked at Ray and was about to say something until he saw Ray's crew walking up.

"Yo fam I don't want no problems." The dude let Tanya go and walked across the club. Tanya turned and looked at Ray.

"Your girl? First of all, I don't know you, so how can I be your girl?"

"Cause I just made you my girl," he said confidently.

Tanya looked at him in disbelief. She thought, *who the fuck he think he is, this nigga think he's the shit*, but Tanya was loving it. But she couldn't let him know that.

"Well I'm sorry sir; I can't be your girl. I don't even know you name."

"It's Ray," he shouted, "Now can you be my girl?"

Just when Tanya was about to answer her cousin Patsy came over, "Wah gwan Yankee", she said to Ray. He laughed "What's good Yardie, dope party."

"Thanks, wah ya fi do over here chatting to my cousin?"

Ray smiled. "Oh word this your cousin? I'm trying to get to know her but she fronting."

Patsy looked at Tanya. "Ya nah like mi fren? Tanya don't be so mean." Patsy whispered in Tanya ear. "Him have money my gyal" Tanya looked at Patsy and laughed. "What's so funny?" Ray said looking at both of them. "Noting mi fren, come buy us a drink." Patsy grabbed Ray and pulled him to the bar. "Please don't go anywhere I'll be right back," he said.

Tanya smiled. She kept dancing until someone tapped her on her shoulder. When she turned around she immediately got annoyed.

"Hey Tee what's up?"

"What's up Bam, what you doing here?" she asked.

"What you mean? You act like I wasn't gonna come support the family. Stop acting like that Tee. Look, what you and La got going on don't have anything to do with me. I knew you since Junior High, so cut the bullshit."

"Whatever Bam! You were right there laughing when he dissed me in front of that bitch from Chester's. But it's all good."

Just then Mary came running up. "LOOK AT MY BITCH!! Tanya what's up?"

"Oh Shit! Mary what's up, who you here with? Where's Kim?"

"Girl I haven't seen Kim in months. I've been O.T."

Tanya looked at Mary; she was fly from head to toe. She was rocking a Salt N Pepa haircut, door knockers with her name in the middle and she was wearing a Le Cote Sportif tracksuit. That's when Tanya realized Mary and Bam was rocking the same suit.

"Wait! Who you came with? BAM?" Tanya asked.

"YESSSS Bitch! That's my man," Mary said rolling her yes. Tanya bust out laughing "since when?" she asked.

Mary looked at Tanya and was getting upset.

Tanya knew Mary couldn't stand Bam. Mary blurted out, "for a minute now. Come here Tanya let me holla at you." Mary grabbed Tanya's arm and pulled her to the side. Mary began to tell details to Tanya about her and Bam. Then she dropped a bomb on Tanya.

"GIRL! When last time you spoke to La?" Mary asked.

"Please, not since that whole drama on Lott street."

Mary wasn't sure if she should tell Tanya this news but, that was her friend and she didn't want her to hear it from somebody else.

"Why you ask?" Tanya asked as she looked at Mary with a strange look.

"Look, I know y'all not together but I know you still love him. La is having a baby from the bitch up in Chester's."

Tanya's heart stopped and her mouth dropped open. *How can he have a baby with her? He said he didn't love her,* she thought. Tanya felt a tear drop to her cheek. Mary looked at her friend and felt bad. "Nah Tee, don't do that here. Fuck that nigga. You can find somebody way better."

Just then Ray walked up. "You good shawty?" He asked while handing her a bottle of champagne. Tanya snapped back into reality. "Yea Yea, I'm good. Just talking to my home girl," before Tanya could say her name Ray shouted, "Mary what the fuck you doing here?"

Tanya and Bam looked at each other and then at Mary. Mary's face was shocked to see Ray at this party. Hoping he didn't blow her up. "Oh hey Ray, This my HOMEGIRL party." Mary gave Ray a look to keep his mouth shut.

"Yo Ma, who this nigga asking you questions?" Bam shouted out.

"What? Nigga who you talking to?" Ray's crew started to walk over.

"Nigga you" Bam stated as his crew started to come as well, "this my fucking girl!"

Ray looked at Mary. Mary's heart was racing. "Babe chill, this my homeboy from back in the days, right Ray?" Ray paused for a second then turned to Bam. "My bad Son, she just my home girl. No Beef."

"And besides Bam, he's with me," Tanya said.

Everybody turned to her.

Ray was stunned for a second but then he began to smile. Mary was confused. "Oh word Tee?" Bam said, "Ok say no more, do you." *Wait till I tell La this shit,* Bam thought to himself. "Babe lets go," Mary walked away but kept looking at Ray. "Later Tee."

"Later."

As they walked away Tanya told Ray "I hope you ready to take care of your new girl," grabbing the spliff from his hand. Ray smiled. "My new girl huh? I don't have a problem doing that."

Tanya looked at Ray. *DAMNNN this nigga look good,* she thought. She was still hurt about what she just heard about La but, it was time for her to move on. "What about your man" Ray asked.

"We been broke up," she said quickly.

Ray was dazed for a second. His thoughts consumed him, *what the fuck was Mary doing there with that clown.*

"Helloo, Hello, Ray? You hear me talking to you?"

"Oh yea shawty. I guess it's on to the next huh?"

Tanya smiled and said "It's on to next....."

Celebration of Life

"YO! Make sure that bar is full with liquor." Latrell was running around for his girl's baby shower. He never thought he would be having a baby with Marsha. It started just him staying there to get his grind on. Now he and Marsha were having a baby boy. He always thought he would only have kids with Tanya. *Damn I miss her,* he thought. But there was no turning back. He grew to love Marsha, anything he asked of her she got done. So he made sure that she was well taking care. If it wasn't for her he wouldn't have had his clientele and he wouldn't be one of the top niggas in Rochester. Today Latrell was gonna make sure Marsha had the best baby shower. He paid for everything. He got DJ SNS to come out and play, cases of Champagne, and the food was catered from her favorite restaurant.

He had a guest list of two hundred people. All his mans from Brooklyn was attending. Everything was coming together. Guest was starting to arrive so Latrell went home to get dress and to pick Marsha up. As soon as he walked in the door Marsha was complaining about everything. "I'm fat, look at my dress, my feet is swollen." She was just saying all of the things that a pregnant woman would say. Latrell walked over to her and tried to calm her down. "Listen Ma, breathe, everything is gonna be fine. You're not fat you're pregnant, and don't worry about your feet, I brought you some Gucci flip flops that you can walk around in ok?" Marsha was relieved that La had everything under control.

She loved him so much but she knew that he didn't love her the same way that she had loved him. She knew he was still in love with his ex, Tanya. A couple of times he said her name in his sleep. The thought of it made her sick to her stomach, but Marsha thought, *Oh well I'm here she's not, I'm carrying his first born, a boy at that, she's not. Fuck that I'm gonna make this nigga love me if it's the last thing I do.*
**

The venue was gorgeous the décor colors was blue and white, a fit setting for a little Prince on the way. "OK Y'ALL. Finally, what we've been waiting for. THE PARENTS TO BE! MARSHA AND LATRELL!!" The DJ yelled. When they walked in everybody clapped and yelled their names. Latrell looked like a Don, he was rocking Burberry from head to toe; Marsha looked so stunning she was wearing a Gucci dress with her Gucci pumps. She wore her hair in a cute bob.

She had her diamond choker on with the bracelet to match and some diamond studs. Marsha was amazed when she saw the place. She was in tears. Latrell did a great job. Marsha turned to La and said "Baby this is beautiful. I'm so happy." "Good, mission complete" he said as he bent down and gave her a kiss. "Now let's go greet our guest and have fun, it's our day Baby." Marsha fell more in love with him. She had everything she wanted from him except his heart but she was determined to get it.

Everybody was having a blast. The DJ was on point with the music. They received so many gifts. They didn't know where all of it would go. The Champagne was flowing; everyone was dancing, tipsy and having a ball. "Yo La this is off the hook." Bam said. Him and Mary came in rocking Guess outfits, looking fly as always. "Thanks bro," La said. "What's good Mary thanks for coming." Mary looked La up and down and then rolled her eyes. "No problem," she said in an annoyed tone.

Latrell laughed. "What's all of that for Mary?" he asked.

"You know you're breaking my home girl heart by having this baby La." She said.

"Look shit happens I'm not doing this here," he said quickly. *Who the fuck Mary think she is?* He thought.

"Yo, mind your fucking business" Bam snapped, "besides didn't Tanya move on with that cornball ass nigga from the Ville."

"WHAT! What nigga?" La questioned.

"Some dude named Ray; I checked into him, he's about his paper, him and his crew. They not in our line of business though."

How can she move on just like that, La's mind started going crazy. The liquor that he was consuming was starting to set in. "Oh word, I'm happy for her. Because I'm happy with my girl," he said.

Marsha came walking over "what y'all over here talking about?" Everybody became quiet. "You girl!" Mary said, "Girl you look gorgeous." La grabbed Marsha and gave her a kiss.

"She's giving me my King," Latrell said confidently. Just then Marsha's cousin, Ramel, came in with his crew. Marsha already saw that Ramel was a bit drunk and she knows how he feels about these New York cats hustling in his town. "I'll be back Babe, let me go greet some guest." Marsha said before she walked over to Ramel.

"Heyy Cuz. I'm glad you came," She gave him a hug but Ramel was acting cold.

He was looking around the venue and saw how it was decorated and how the bar was stocked with all of the liquor and champagne. In his mind he said, *this motherfucker paid a good chunk of money for this baby shower. These New York cats coming in my town and eating and I can't eat? All that is about to change.*

"Ramel. Helloo," Marsha called out.

"Sorry Marsh. This is real nice y'all doing real good over here huh?"

"Ramel don't start, the whole family is here. Please, I don't want any drama." Marsha was nervous because she knew how her cousin was. "Nah I'm good," he reassured her.

But you see that wasn't true, Ramel and his boys came to stick up some New York cats. He got the word that they were coming for this event. He had been watching their every move since they got in town. He even put some of his home girls on them to keep them busy.

"La, what up Son," Ramel stepped to Latrell. Latrell wasn't too fond of him because he already knew that he was a grimy ass nigga.

"What up Ra, thanks for coming. This my bro Bam."

Bam looked at Ramel with a screwed face as he just nodded his head. Bam knew a couple of niggas like Ramel, them jealous ass niggas who wanna be down. So he already knew to be on point. "What's good fam" Ramel said. He turned back to La, "damn son you must have spent ten stacks on this baby shower, shit looking right in here. I thought I was in a Puff Daddy event."

Ramel's mans started laughing but La didn't think it was funny. He knew Ramel was clocking his pocket. "Well, look I thank y'all for coming but I really want Marsha to enjoy this day without any drama feel me?" Latrell looked at Ramel with a serious face. *Nigga come in my baby shower drunk as fuck. With his goons,* he thought. None of them was dressed for the occasion. So he knew what kind of time they were on. La gave Bam the look but Bam was on point already.

Feeling like he was being dismissed and disrespected, Ramel started getting loud. "What you saying La? Me and my team got to go? Nigga you in my town, if it wasn't for my cousin you wouldn't be making any type of money. My nigga you in my town! Y'all young ass New Yorkers think you can come and take over… fuck outta here."

Ramel took a swing at Latrell but missed. Latrell laughed and grabbed Ramel. "YO Son! On the real I'm gonna act like that didn't happen. Ramel do you remember when I first came down here I tried to plug you in. I gave you a Q.P of some greens and what did you do Ra? You smoked my shit and fronted like you got robbed. My nigga you had me on a goose chase for niggas that didn't exist. So you really think I'm gonna put you down with my team after that bullshit?"

La bust out laughing, "nigga you a clown. Get out my shit. I don't need any scenes." Just then Ramel punched La in his face and all hell broke loose. Latrell and Ramel started fighting. With no hesitation Bam jumped in stomping Ramel on the ground. Ramel's right hand man came and bust Bam in the head with a bottle. Mary saw that and went off. Taking her blade from her purse, she walked up to dude from behind and sliced him across his cheek. Marsha started screaming and crying. The rest of her family began to jump in. So now it was Rochester against New York City.

Two bitches jumped on Mary, pulling her hair. But Mary already knew to at least hold one bitch down. Mary was swinging her blade from left to right. Everybody in the baby shower was damn near fighting. Marsha started screaming louder. All of a sudden shots rang out. Everybody scattered all over. Ramel took cover as well as Latrell. Latrell just remembered. "OH SHIT! MARSHA," he said. He got up and started calling her name; he was looking all over for her but couldn't find her. Just then Mary let out a big scream and called La.

"LA, LA HURRY PLEASE! SHE'S OVER HERE!!" La ran to where Mary was and when he looked down all he saw was blood, so much blood. Marsha was crying. "Baby, please help me" she said to him. La was stuck in a daze.

Bam ran over, "OH SHIT! OH SHIT!" he repeated "La we have to get her to a hospital. LAAAAA" Bam screamed, "Snap the fuck out of it!! The baby La."

La looked back towards the floor and dropped to his knees. "Baby where are you shot?" he asked. Out of breath Marsha said, "La my stomach, the baby La, the baby." Tears began to come down his cheeks. "CALL THE AMBULANCE MARSHA BEEN SHOT, CALL THE AMBULANCE!!!!!!!!!!" he screamed.

Ramel stood up from his hiding place and ran over. "COUSIN I'M SORRY. OH MY GOD!" Bam grabbed him by his neck. "Nigga this is your fault. One of your mans did this. None of us was strapped." Ramel was in shock. "If something happens to my man's son and Marsha, be prepared for a war," Bam was livid.

"BAM!!! NOT RIGHT NOW!" Mary yelled, "La needs us." Latrell held Marsha in his arms, "Baby hold on they coming," La said. Marsha looked at Latrell, oh how she loved him. "La save the baby please," she cried.

"Shhhh y'all gonna be alright. WHERE THE FUCK IS THE AMBULANCE? Bam get the car we gotta take her."

La looked at Marsha, she was closing her eyes. "NO BABY, keep your eyes open, look at me."

"Baby it's cold, I'm cold," she said.

Latrell couldn't wait, he picked her up and began to run to the car, Bam and Mary was right behind him. Bam opened the car door. Latrell laid her in the back seat and put her head on his lap. Bam was driving like a crazy man.

"HURRY, PLEASE BAM!!" La cried, "Don't worry baby, we almost there," La said to a bleeding Marsha.

La looked down at Marsha; her eyes were closed as if she was sleeping peacefully.

"BABY... BABY... WAKE UP!!! BAM HURRY!"

Mary started crying. Bam felt so bad for his friend. La did a big scream and then called her name.

"MARSHA!!!!!!"

WHAT THE FUCK!!

Ray and his mans sat in the car in shock. They just looked at all the drama that was going. Ray's thoughts started to turn rapidly, *"What the fuck Mary got me into,"* he thought. As Ray and his mans continued to watch everybody running out of the baby shower, he finally saw the people that he'd been waiting for. But what he saw in front of him had him more in shock and confused.

"What the fuck Ray?" Nick said, "What your sister getting us into?"

Ray watched as Latrell carried Marsha in his arms. He was all covered in blood. Mary and Bam followed right behind him. They both jumped in the car with La and then sped off.

"Follow them" Ray said.

Nick drove two cars behind them, hoping they wouldn't be seen. Bam's car made a sudden stop.

"Pull in right here and let's just sit and wait" Ray said.

"Ray you sure you still wanna go through with this? Shit just looking too crazy" Nick said nervously.

"Look, I didn't come all the way the fuck out here to turn around."

"Look I understand that, but Ray this shit look crazy. Police soon gonna be popping up. I didn't come all the way da fuck up here to get locked up," Nick said seriously.

"CHILL MY NIGGA!" My Sister wouldn't put me in harm's way. She said tonight was the night since all these cats are in town. Now the plan is still in effect," Ray was shouting. *Let me call Mary and see what the fuck is going,* Ray thought as he reached for his phone.

**

Mary sat in the hospital in total shock. She couldn't believe what really took place. She kept playing it over and over in her head.

Mary's thoughts were interrupted by the vibration of her phone. She fumbled through her purse for the phone. "Shit Ray" she whispered. She totally forgot that tonight was the night that they intended to execute their plan. Mary looked up and saw Bam consoling his friend. So many thoughts ran through her head. *Damn, I feel sorry for La. Bam is so good to me, everything that I ask for I always receive.* Mary caught herself getting emotional. *NOPE, NOPE, I can't allow myself to fall for him,*

He's a good dude, but not for long. Sorry Bam this is business, her thoughts were running a mile a minute.

"Ma'am? Excuse me Ma'am"

Mary looked up at the nurse, "yes?"

"You need to be seen for your injuries, you're losing a lot of blood." Mary looked at her arm and saw two big slashes. She didn't even realize she was cut. She was starting to feel numbness in her fingers. The nurse took her to a room to work on her.

**

"Bro I need you to calm down she's gonna be alright." Bam was trying to calm Latrell but it wasn't working

"FUCK, FUCK, FUCK" La screamed out, "Why her? I swear Bro if something happens to Marsha or my baby, I'm murdering her cousin."

"Yo La, all jokes aside shit about to get real after this. We have to prepare ourselves. I'm gonna tell Nu Black to move the weight to the stash spot. Niggas is on our heads now Bro. Be prepared to exit this town." La looked at Bam and knew he was right. But he refused to go back to Brooklyn to live with Marsha and the baby. *Maybe we will go to Virginia or something,* he thought.

Just then Marsha's mother and sister came running in. "WHERE'S MY BABY!! I WANNA SEE MY BABY!!" Marsha's mother cried, "La where is she?" Latrell hugged Ms. Graham and said "she in surgery Ma, calm down. We have to wait to see if she and the baby are okay." Bam looked at Latrell and couldn't take all of this. Mary came walking out of the room just in the nick of time. "Babe I wanna go home," Mary was drugged up from the meds they gave her. Plus, her head was pounding from Ray that kept calling. "It's too much going on right now. We have to execute our plan. La we out. I'm gonna take care of what we discussed. I'll hit you up before I go to your spot. Hold ya head Bro," Bam said as he grabbed Mary's hand and left.

**

Meanwhile, Ray fell asleep waiting for Mary to exit the hospital. Nick began to doze off too. Just when he was about to close his eyes again, he saw Mary and Bam leaving the hospital.

"RAY! RAY! WAKE UP!"

Ray jumped up, "what the fuck you screaming for?" he asked. Nick pointed to their target. "OK, Nigga its show time."

Nick drove behind Bam. Bam was so out of it that he didn't
even notice the car following them.

"Babe, we're leaving Rochester, Shit is hot now. Look just in
case I have to leave before you, here's the keys to the stash
house on Cooper. I need you to grab what's there, I don't trust
these motherfuckers," Bam said with a serious voice. Mary
was out of it but she heard everything that Bam had just said.
*Damn he's making me feel bad about my plan, but fuck it he
has to get it,* Mary thought. "I love you Babe remember that,"
Bam turned to her and said. Mary looked at him. "I Love you
Bam."

**

"We're home Babe. Nu Black should be in the house, I
sent him to go pick up a grand somebody owed and Rich
should be here too, I sent him to pick some work and cash
from one of the stash houses. It's time to close shop". When
they walked in the house Rich was counting the money that he
had just picked up. On the floor was fifteen pounds of weed.
"What up Rich?"
"Hey Bro"
"What's good Mary? You alright" Rich asked.
"Yea in a little pain but I'll be good."

Mary went in the room to get her things together. Ray stopped calling so she didn't know where he was. She was hoping he left so that they could do this another day. Mary went in the closest, took her MCM duffle bag out and filled it up with the money she was saving. Every time Bam gave her money she put it up. Majority of the time she took money from his stash. Bam was making so much money that he didn't even notice. She even put away five pounds of weed; she had him thinking he lost it somewhere.

She began to pack her clothes in another bag with her shoes and jewelry. She went to the garage to put her things in her Jeep Cherokee that Bam had just bought her. As she was coming back in the house she heard a knock on the door. "That must be Nu-Black" Bam said. "Okay Babe I'm going to take a shower to wash this blood off of me," Mary said. She then started walking towards the bathroom.

There was a knock at the door again, "Damn Black, one minute."

When Bam opened the door he saw the tip of a .45 pointed at him. "NO Nigga! It ain't Black," Ray said. Bam's eyes opened wide. "WHAT THE FUCK NIGGA? YOU MUST HAVE LOST YOUR MIND!!"

Rich jumped up with his peace in his hand and pointed it at Ray. Just then Nick came in and busted two shots, hitting Rich in the leg. Ray turned around and hit Bam in the head with his gun. Bam hit the floor and his blood squirted everywhere. Mary heard the shots and began to cry, she quickly locked the bathroom door. She didn't know who it was.

She didn't think it was Ray. She figured it was these Chester Cats. "That's it I'm dead. Lord if I shall die let it be quick," Mary prayed to herself. Someone started banging on the door.

"GET THE FUCK OUT!" the voice said, "I'M GIVING YOU TO THE COUNT OF THREE THEN I'M GONNA START SHOOTING… 1, 2…"

Mary opened the door "DON'T SHOOT, DON'T SHOOT," she screamed. Nick grabbed Mary by her hair. Mary didn't know him so she just knew in her head that it was the Chester boys coming to kill them. "YO, don't touch my fucking girl!" Bam shouted. Ray laughed. Bam kept looking at Ray, *this nigga look too familiar. Where do I know from?* Bam thought to himself.

Nick came out the back with Mary half naked and threw her on the floor. "YOO, chill don't be so ruff," Ray said. Mary looked up and was relieved when she saw Ray. "RAY! Thank god, I thought it was these clowns from out here."

FUCKING RAY? Tanya shorty? Nah I know Tee didn't send these niggas out here to get at La. Tee wouldn't do that, Bam thought. "What the fuck you want Nigga? Why you out here? And Bitch why you so happy to see him," Bam screamed at Mary. Ray hit Bam in the mouth with his gun. "Watch your fucking mouth don't ever talk to my sister like that." "SISTER? Mary what is he talking about?" Bam asked.

Ray helped Mary off of the floor. "Oh let me sit back and let baby sis explain," Ray said. Mary stood up feeling dizzy, still high off of the meds. She looked at Bam and part of hurt felt bad but her loyalty wasn't to him. "Remember when you did that robbery on Linden Boulevard? That was your big come up, the start of your new life. Your new life out here. Well that night was my worst nightmare."

Bam was confused.

"How me robbing the Jamaicans was your worst nightmare? Mary what the fuck you talking about?" Bam asked.

"You remember when you went into that spot and you saw that beautiful girl in there. She was begging you not to kill her."

Bam's heart started racing as he listened to Mary talk. He started thinking about Kisha. "You told your mans to kill her, you left a poor hopeless body on the floor," she said with sad eyes.

83

"How the fuck you know all of this Mary, and what does she has to do with you?" Bam asked. Ray got up and kicked him in the mouth. Bam's two front teeth came out, "SHUT THE FUCK UP NIGGA!!" Bam held his mouth as the blood poured out. Bam's phone started to ring, it was La. He called ten times back to back, then paged him 911 911. Mary continued to talk, "I'll tell what she has to do with me. See what you didn't know Bam is that she was my sister, Ray's twin."

Bam's eyes opened wide, "Babe I didn't know I'm sorry." Mary started crying, "DON'T BABE ME!! She was my heart, my only sister. I had to get you back. So I became your girl and pretended to love you so that I could find out everything. I planned out everything for this moment right here." Bam was so heated. He wondered how he could fall for her like that. He figured he must have truly loved this girl. "YOU FUCKING BITCH!! After all I did for you!" Bam shouted. "Oh yes thank you... thank you for all of that. Straight bonuses for me," Mary said quickly.

"YO, I'm tired of hearing all this crying shit. Nick bag that up, the weed and the money," Ray said as his thoughts consumed him. He thought he hit the jackpot. "Sis go put some clothes on. Let me tie this nigga up." Mary ran towards the back of the house and threw on some clothes. She went to the closet and took three duffle bags out of money and drugs. She left one bag in there for Ray to find. *Fuck that, I put in all the hard work, fucking and sucking this nigga off. It's my turn to shine. What Ray don't know won't hurt him,* she thought as she snuck out the backdoor to put the bags in her trunk.

Rich started to come to after passing out. He gave Bam the look and reached for his gun. Ray and Nick was too busy searching out the house. Rich sat up a little just then Nick turned around and saw Rich moving. By the time he reached for his nine Rich shot two shots both bullets hit Nick. One in the arm and one in the stomach. Rich jumped up to run out the back door. When he ran to the back he grabbed Mary. "Mary, let's go before they kill you," he pulled her arm. Mary snatched away and quickly pulled out a .45. She told Rich, "you not going anywhere." She shot him dead in the head. Ray called Mary's name out. When she walked out of the back he was relieved.

Bam couldn't believe what he was seeing. "Mary I'm sorry. I'll give you anything. I'm good for it, you know that," Bam said. "Sorry Babe. Just like you told your man when my sister was begging for her life," Mary turned to Ray and then continued, "Finish him." Ray put two bullets in Bam's head. Bam's eyes were wide open looking at Mary.

"Let's go Ray…" Mary said.

"You can't leave Sis. You have to stay. If you leave they gonna know you was down with it."

"Ray I don't wanna stay here."

"You have no choice. I'll see you back at home in a few. Now this is gonna hurt a little…"

Ray shot Mary in the arm. Just as Nu-Black was gonna open the door he heard a shot and Mary scream. He ran back to his car and drove away. "FUCK! Damn cuz." He drove in silence for a few blocks and then he looked down at the bag full of money and drugs and bust out laughing. "IT'S MY TURN TO SHINE BABY!!! N.C HERE I COME…" he said eagerly as he grinned.

Mary fell to the floor next to Bam. Ray grabbed the bags and helped Nick to the car. He then came back in the house and said, "Sis I will hold your cut till you get home."

"Ray help I'm in pain," she said as she grabbed her bleeding arm.

"Don't worry I'll call the police on my throw away. You'll be fine." Ray then closed the door behind him. Mary looked at Bam's lifeless body. "I'm sorry Bam," she whispered as her eyes began to close…

Back Together Again

Tanya had been texting and calling Kim for three days. She knew Kim was upset because Tanya missed her graduation ceremony. Tanya knew she was wrong for that, but ever since Ray came back from out of town he's been around her 24/7. Since he got another crib in Park Slope they had been too busy shopping for the apartment. He even brought her a new Gucci bag with a pair of sneakers to match. Things just felt like they were moving too fast. She felt like she was running away from something. Tanya needed a break from him, so she went to visit her mom in Flatbush. She decided to walk to Tennis Court to see if Kim was home.

Tennis was crowded everybody was chilling on the block. As always, the niggas was gambling in front of the castle. Quincy was flipping on one of his mans for cheating. "My nigga run my money, you always ass betting!" Mark laughed, "Chill son I got you keep rolling my nigga." "Yo Mark! I don't have time for games. If you don't give me my bread I'm gonna fuck you up." "Damn Q, really over a hundred bucks," Mark said.

"You fucking right. Your ass always trying to cheat somebody. Give me my shit!!!" Quincy said as he held his hand out.

"Here my nigga, Here you fucking cry baby," Mark said as he handed Quincy the money.

Everybody started to laugh.

"I don't give a fuck it's my bread," Quincy said as he began to count the bills.

Tanya up walked to Quincy, "Hey Q, what's good?"

"Tanya what's up? Long time no see. Those Brownsville niggas got you hostage? You don't come around anymore."

Tanya felt bad, "shut up where's your sister?"

"She walked around the corner to the pizza shop. She been around there for a minute," Quincy said.

"I'll walk to see if I see her. If she comes back tell her I'm out here," Tanya said.

"Got you T."

**

Tanya walked to the pizza shop. When she walked in she didn't see Kim. As soon as she was about to walk out she heard Kim's laugh. Tanya walked to the back of the pizza shop and there was Kim. She couldn't see the dude she was

with but she could see that Kim was all smiles and blushing.
Kim looked up and saw Tanya. Her eyes opened like she saw
a ghost. Tyreek looked at Kim, "What's wrong Babe?" he
asked. When he turned around he saw Tanya standing there.
Tanya's mouth dropped when she noticed Tyreek's face.
"Hey Tanya what's going on?" he got up to greet Tanya.
Kim was still in shock to see her. Kim had been seeing
Tyreek for some time now. She wanted to keep it on the low.
"What's good T?" Kim finally said
"Hello Kim can I speak to you for a minute? Excuse us Ty"

Tanya grabbed Kim by her hand and took her outside.
"What the hell is going on?" Tanya yelled, "Bitch since when
you was seeing Tyreek?"
"For a while now," Kim said with an attitude, "and why the
fuck you care. You haven't been around. Yo ass been
underneath Ray's ass. You can't answer my fucking calls. You
missed my graduation and mad other shit. So don't come over
here and question me."
Tanya felt like shit. Everything Kim was saying was right she
haven't been around. "Damn Kim, I'm sorry. I know I fucked
up. Please forgive me. I bought you a graduation gift."

Kim tried to act mad but she cracked a smile as she
opened the box Tanya gave her. "YOOO these are dope T!"
Tanya gave Kim some door knocker earrings with her name in

the middle. "Thank You! Thank You T!" She hugged her best friend. "I missed you Kim! It's so much shit I have to tell you."

"Girl me too," Kim said.

"Well I'm staying in Flatbush tonight come by my mom's. She's at work so you can spend a night," Tanya said.

"Ok, let me go back inside. I'll see you later," Kim said.

Kim walked inside and heard Tyreek on the phone. "Yo relax it's taking some time but I'm working on it. Don't worry it's gonna happen." Tyreek turned around and saw Kim standing there. "I'll call you later," he told the person on the phone.

"Hey Babe. How long were you standing there?" Tyreek asked nervously.

"Enough," Kim said, "Who was that?" she asked.

"Yo my man, he want me to help him with a project," Tyreek switched the conversation quick. "What Tanya talking about?" he asked.

"Oh nothing she bought me a graduation gift," Kim said as she showed off her earrings.

"That's cool." Tyreek said, "We never celebrated you graduating. We should do something. Go out to eat to Mr. Chows in the city. Go to the club after. My man Travis having a birthday party at the Tunnel next Sunday."

"What Travis? From Ocean?" she asked.

"Yea you know him?" Tyreek asked.

"Yea he hang out with my brother from time to time plus his sister is my home girl."

"Oh okay cool. So we all set. I really wanna spend some alone time with you Kim," Tyreek grabbed Kim's hand.

Kim started to feel nervous. *How do I tell him I'm a virgin?* She thought. "Look I want you to be my girl. I was feeling you since school. I only want to be with you if you let me." Kim's heart melted to his words. She was open off of Tyreek. Every time he touched her she would get a tingle between her legs. "Do you wanna be my girl Kim?" he asked. "Yes," Kim answered quickly feeling embarrassed. Tyreek smiled. "Come here Babe." Kim came close to him. Tyreek kissed Kim long and slow.

She became so wet she didn't know what to do. Tyreek looked Kim in her eyes and said, "You're mines." Kim blushed. "Are you going to Tanya's?" he asked.

"Yes. I'm spending the night," Kim replied.

"Can I come see you over there before you go to sleep?" he asked.

"Yes Babe," Kim said as she smiled. Tyreek winked his eye.

"Good, see you later," he said.

They both went their separate ways. Kim was walking home smiling. She finally had her man.

Sweetest Thing

Tanya was preparing dinner for her and Kim. Tanya could throw down in the kitchen. She had her music blasting. She was rocking out to some Faith Evans. Tanya was making oxtails with peas and rice. One of Kim's favorite dishes. The bell buzzed. Tanya ran to the door. "Who is it?' she asked eagerly.

"Who you think it is," Kim shouted.

Tanya buzzed her in. Kim came up stairs. "Girl you knew it was only me," Kim said as they both laughed. "Damn T that shit smells good. Is it done?" Kim asked as she licked her lips.

"In a few. Bitch you just walked in the door. Take your coat off. I got some Remy and some bud," Tanya said.

"You really into your bud," Kim said.

"It keeps me mellow," Tanya explained, "bitch stop acting like you never smoked."

"Oh I never said that. Me and Tyreek smoke all the time"

"Excuse me, you and Tyreeeeeeek," Tanya teased.

"Shut up bitch," Kim laughed.

"Nah seriously, how the hell you link up with Tyreek," Tanya questioned.

"Girl me and Janay were downtown getting some shit for my graduation. We walked in Albee Square Mall and we see him and his mans buying some gold fronts. Janay said, let's walk over there. At first I was fronting, like for what? So Janay was like, girl you don't see Tyreek over with his friends let's go say hi. Just when I was gonna say no she grabbed my arm and pulled me."

Tanya rolled her eyes, "her feen out ass."
They both laughed. "Anyways," Kim said, "we walk over there and Janay was all loud saying hi so Tyreek turned around and Tanya I'm not gonna even lie, my mouth dropped."
"Why?" Tanya asked, "He looked fucked up?"
Kim looked at Tanya, "fucked up? Fucked up where that nigga looked good as hell. Girl all I heard was Lauren Hill in my head."
Tanya was confused. "Lauren Hill?"
"Yesss!" Kim yelled, "Lauren Hill." Then Kim began to sing:

"Sweetest thing I've ever known
Was like a kiss on a collarbone
The soft caress of happiness
The way you walk, your style of dress

I wish I didn't get so weak

Oooh, baby, just to hear you speak….

"Kim, Kim, HELLOOOO KIM!!" Tanya yelled. Kim stopped singing and looked at Tanya. "What??" she said. "Nobody wants to hear your fucking singing! Get back to telling the story already," Tanya said feeling annoyed. "Alright, Alright T. So anyway Tyreek came over. He said hi to us, you know small talk, and then he asked if he could talk to me for a minute. He pulled me to the side. He said: "I have been looking for you for a minute. I even went on your block looking for you but I didn't ask anybody for you. You know how those people are over there. Anyways, I wanna take you out to the movies or something. I wanna get to know you."

Girl you know I was hype. So we exchanged numbers and the rest is history. We chill every day. He talks to me when I fall asleep on the phone. It's the best girl," Kim said. Tanya turned to her friend "that sounds cute but what I wanna know is… Bitch did you fuck him?" Tanya blurted out. "NOOO!" Kim put her head down and said "I'm scared," she admitted.

"Bitch you didn't tell him you're a virgin?"

"No," Kim felt ashamed.

"Shit me and Ray be fucking down the place," Tanya laughed, "shit the first time we had sex was in his car on Belmont Ave. Right in front his building. I'm not gonna lie a bitch was scared but I was so high and tipsy. I didn't want him to stop. Girl he put his hands down my pants, I was soak and wet. I told him let's go upstairs. He said he wanted it right then and there. He pulled my pants down moved my panties to the side and gurrrrl. I was in heaven. He did things Latrell never did. Look if you're looking for a fairytale type of night it may not happen like that. You just have to go with the flow Kim. Just relax and breathe. Now if you're feeling uncomfortable then let him go on your own pace."

Tanya paused to catch her breath before she continued. "Bitch I'm hungry let's eat and get these drinks going I really did miss my best friend." Kim smiled but her mind was on Tyreek. She really wanted him to be her first. She had falling in love with him and she knew that's who she was gonna be with for the rest of her life.

Tanya and Kim ate, smoked, drank, danced and sung to every song that came on the radio.

They were interrupted by Kim's phone ringing. "Hello?" Kim answered.

"Hey Babe, what you doing?" Tyreek asked with his deep tone, Kim felt excited once she heard his voice.

"Nothing chilling, listening to music and talking" she said.

"I wanna see you. Come down stairs," he ordered.

"Hold on," Kim said. "Oh my God he's down stairs, he wants me to come down T," Kim whispered to Tanya.

"Tell him to come upstairs my moms not here. He can come up," Tanya said.

Kim went back on the phone, "you can come up stairs Tanya mother not here. Press bell 2B."

"Okay I'll be there in three minutes," he said.

"Okay" Kim said as she rushed off the phone.

"He'll be here three minutes," Kim said to Tanya. She was feeling all excited and nervous. "Well bitch go freshen up. You over here smelling like a bottle of Remy," Tanya said as they laughed. "When he comes I will open the door for him," she added.

Kim went to get ready. Tyreek buzzed the bell and Tanya let him up. When she opened the door, Tyreek was standing there. Tanya thought, *Damn Kim was right, he is the sweetest thing.*

"Hey T. Where's Kim?" Tyreek asked.

"Hey Ty, she's in the bathroom. Come in, you want a drink?"

"What y'all drinking?" He asked.

"Remy. You want some?"

"Sure," he said gladly. "So where you been T I haven't been seeing you around?" he asked.

"I be with my shawty in Brownsville," Tanya responds.

Just then Kim came out the bathroom. Tyreek smiled, he really was feeling Kim. She was perfect to him, her shape, and her skin tone. She had long beautiful hair. *My little Spanish Mami,* he thought. When Kim saw Tyreek she smiled. *Damn he looks good from head to toe,* she thought. Tyreek's height was 5'10. He was light skin with hazel eyes. He was bow legged and well built. "You look nice Babe," Kim said. Ty had on a Guess jean suit with a Polo sweater and some construction Timbs on. His hair was cut short with waves. Kim walked up to him gave him a hug. Tanya gave him the drink, "now if you want something else ask your GIRL to get it," she said.

They laughed. Tanya went in her room to give them privacy plus she was tired. Kim's heart started racing. They were finally alone. "You look nice. Where are you going?" Kim asked. "To the Kit Kat Club. Big Don having a party in there, me and the crew going," Tyreek replied. Kim took a sip of the Remy; she was already feeling drunk thinking about what Tanya said, *just go with the flow.* Kim moved closer to Tyreek. She wrapped her hands around his neck. "Can I ask you a question Tyreek?"

"Yes Babe. You okay?" Tyreek was afraid she was gonna ask about that call from earlier.

"You really want me to be yours?"

Tyreek smiled, "no doubt!"

Kim began to kiss Tyreek. He started feeling all over her body. He put his hands under her shirt and began to play with her nipples. Kim began to let out soft moans. "You sure you want to do this Kim?" Tyreek asked her.

"Yes," she whispered in-between moans. He unbuttoned her pants and slid his hands down her panties. He began to play with her clit he was amazed at how wet she was. Kim began to moan even loader. "Babe be quiet. Tanya's in the next room," Tyreek whispered. Kim bit down on her bottom lip. Her body started feeling weird. She couldn't explain it. Tyreek kept rubbing on her and kissing her. He wanted her so bad. His dick was about to bust out his pants. Kim's body began to tremble.

Just when she thought she was about to cum Tyreek's phone rang. Causing him to stop, "Yo, Gee what up?" Ty answered, "Alright I'm coming down now."

"Babe I gotta go" Tyreek said as he stood from the couch. Kim didn't want him to leave. She put on a sad face. "Don't do that," Ty said, "plus I don't want to do this on Tanya's couch you're better than that. I'll tell you what, since we have plans Sunday to go to dinner and to The Tunnel I'll get us a room. Tell your father that you're staying with Tanya again. Okay Babe?"

Kim looked at him with sad eyes. She wanted him to stay but he was right, she didn't want her first time like this anyway. "Ok Ty," she said. He gave her a kiss and told her that he would call her later. Kim closed the door behind him and then went to lie on the couch. She was horny like a dog. She couldn't wait until Sunday. She kept thinking about Ty and how she was falling in love with him. As she was closing her eyes she thought, *I hope Sunday will be a night to remember.*

Making Moves

Kim woke up because her cell was ringing.

"Hello?"

"Hey Kimmy, its Daddy. Are you up yet?" Luke asked.

"No dad. What's up?" she asked.

"I need you to make some moves today for me. I need you to pick up some money in Canarsie and in Brownsville for me."

"Okay Dad," Kim said.

Luke was on a mission. A lot of people owed him money and it was time to collect. The number business was going good. Some nights weren't, but he still was making money. On Friday and Saturday nights he would run a big poker game and have a dice game running in one of the other rooms. The around the way hustlers was always in there. Luke had a fully stocked bar, while they gambled they could buy drinks. On Saturdays Ms. Sheryl would sell dinner plates to whoever was gambling.

"Kim. You and Tanya can do that early for me. I got y'all when you get back."

"Okay Dad. We are getting up now."

Kim hung up the phone and sat up. Tanya was already up in the kitchen. Kim walked in the kitchen. "Good Morning, Kim you hungry?" Tanya asked.

"Shit! Hell yea!" Kim said, "Oh Luke wants us to make some moves for him he said he got us when we come back. We have to go to Canarsie and Brownsville."

"Okay, when we go to the Ville I can stop and check on my crib and see if Ray been there. Plus I can pick up some stuff to take to the other crib" Tanya said.

"Cool," Kim said, "well let's get this day started. I wanna go to King's Plaza to get some stuff for Sunday."

"What's Sunday?" Tanya question, "what's Sunday?"

"Oh yea, Tyreek said Travis from Ocean Ave having a party in The Tunnel. You know the whole Flatbush gonna be in there. He told me to come since we didn't celebrate my graduation. And then we gonna get a hotel room after."

Tanya's eyes opened up wide. "Girl you finally gonna give it up huh?" Tanya asked. Kim busted out laughing, "Shut the fuck up T. I wanted to give it to him last night but he went out plus he said he didn't want to do it on your couch not for our first time. So I wanna go to the mall and get some things to look nice for him."

Tanya smiled, "Okay Kim. I'm coming with you to The Tunnel maybe Ray wanna go. It's gonna be poppin. You know Quincy and the crew gonna shut it down," Tanya said.

"As always. You know my brothers are fly," Kim bragged.

"I knowwwww why you never hooked a bitch up with one of them," Tanya asked. Kim laughed, "Bitch get out my face and get dress we have a lot to do," Kim said in a joking manner.
**

Kim and Tanya headed out to Canarsie first. They went to pick up fifteen hundred from Ms. Carter.

"Good Afternoon Ms. Carter my father told me to stop by," Kim said.

"Oh Yes! Hold on Baby," Ms. Carter came back with an envelope full of money. "Here Baby tell your father I cooked him a meal and brought him some cigarettes back from Maryland. Tell him put these numbers in for midday and evening," Ms. Carter said.

"Ok Ms. Carter," Kim said, she was in a rush to leave. Ms. Carter was the kind of woman that if you didn't leave she would talk your ear off. "Ok, Ok Ms. Carter, I got to go." Ms. Carter was still talking as Kim walked away. "Tell your father to call me."

When Kim got back in the car she burst out laughing. "What the fuck is all of this I thought we were picking up money," Tanya said. Kim looked at Tanya. "Girl I don't know what Luke do to these ladies. They always sending him gifts," Kim said. Tanya laughed out loud "they better stop before Maria come chop them up with her machete!" Kim laughed, "for real my mom will wild out on these bitches for Luke." "Yo! Since we in Canarsie let's just go to Kings Plaza and get our outfits and get something to eat. I have to make an appointment with Suzette for my hair," Kim said. "Yes me too." Tanya replied, "tell her we both coming early."

Kim and Tanya finally got to Kings Plaza. The Mall was crowded. Kings Plaza was always the hangout spot. They walked in The Gap and picked some jeans and a varsity jacket. While they was in there they bumped into the twins. Now the twins was the truth when it came down to boosting anything you wanted they could get. "What's up girls? What y'all in here getting?" they asked.

"Oh some jeans and the new varsity jackets. You can help us?" Kim asked. The twins looked at each other and then at Kim and said, "we got you. Meet us by the cookie shop in half an hour."

Kim smiled, "okay we going to two more stores then we'll meet you." The twins went to do what they did best while Kim and T went into Victoria's Secret to get some new underwear. "Look Kim you have to get sexy it's your first time and you saying you really feeling him. You got to show and prove. Plus, I need to get me some new things for me and Ray," Tanya said. They both picked an outfit plus new bras and panties. They then went next door and bought dresses for the night. Kim bought this sexy red Guess dress with some black pumps. Tanya bought a pink one to match Kim's with some black pumps. They just knew they were gonna be the shit at the party on Sunday. "Oh shit we gotta meet the twins," Kim said.

They left out of the store to meet with the twins at the cookie shop. The twins got their jackets plus a couple of jeans a piece. "How much we owe you?" Tanya asked.

"A movie date," Marcus said.

Tanya laughed and said. "A date?"

Michael said, "Yea. We want to take y'all out. We want to chill with y'all."

Tanya looked at Kim and then looked at the twins before she began to talk, "ok bet! Give me y'all numbers. We gonna call y'all when we ready to go."

Kim's eyes opened up looking at Tanya thinking, *this bitch done lost her mind, she must've forgot that I'm with Tyreek and that she's with Ray.* The twins were hype. They gave each other pounds while they walked into Macy's. "Yo let's get something to eat then off to Brownsville we go," Tanya said. The girls chilled in Nathan's for a while. They were just cracking jokes and looking over all of the things they got. Just then they saw a bunch of cops running into the mall. "What the hell?" Kim said, "I wonder who they coming for?" Tanya said, "I hope it ain't the twins."

Just then the police was walking by with two suspects. The twins got caught in Macy's stealing leather coats. Michael turned his head and saw Kim and Tanya. He put his head down quickly. Kim and Tanya were in shock. "Well Kim, now you don't have to worry about that date" Tanya said. They burst out laughing. "Let's make our way to The Ville," Tanya said, "your father will soon call for his money."
**

Tanya opened the door to her and Ray's apartment. It was so silent. The table had light dust on it. They haven't been here in weeks since they moved to Park Slope.
"This apartment is big T. What you need a three bedroom for?" Kim asked. "This used to be Ray's mother apartment but she left it to him when she moved to V.A. I'll be back let me get my things," Tanya said. Tanya went in the room got

something out of the draw and went into the closet. She took some things out that she wanted to take to the other apartment. She saw one of Ray's leather jackets. "Oh let me take this for Ray," she mumbled.

As soon as Tanya grabbed the jacket, a zip lock bag full of jewelry fell out of the pocket. Tanya picked up the bag "what the fuck is Ray doing with all of this jewelry" she said out loud. She opened it. It had two Gucci links, a Rolex watch, a Cartier watch, diamond studs, some door knockers and three finger rings. One ring caught her eye. "What the fuck? Bam? Why the hell he has a ring that says Bam?" she mumbled. "Maybe it's one of his mans there can be two niggas named Bam. I will ask him about the jewelry when I see him."

She put the bag up in the closet and took the jacket. "Ready Kim?" Tanya asked once she entered the living room. Kim was looking at the pictures on the wall. "Yo this little girl in this picture looks familiar. It's like I seen this picture before" Kim said.
"Girl you know everybody has someone that looks like them. All light skin people look alike," Tanya replied jokingly. Kim said, "you sure right about that. Let's roll T."
**

Kim and Tanya walked in Luke's spot. It was crowded as usual. Niggas and bitches was at the table playing pitty pat another table had the spades going the next table had the dominoes plus people were putting in their numbers for the evening. Kim walked in the back room where the dice game was going on. "What up Kim" one of the guys from the hood said. "What's up? You saw my father?" she said. "Hey, he went to his office" the guy said.

"Thanks" she said as she walked out.

**

"Yo Son! What's shorty name?" A next dude asked.

"That's Kim, Luke's daughter why?" the guy asked.

"KIM? I know her." The guy said.

"Nigga what you talking about? Hassan don't come fucking around, Luke will kill you for his daughter!"

"Please no he won't. That's my future wife," Hassan said. Everybody looked at him and laughed.

"Nigga relax. Her brothers ain't having that shit either you know how many niggas tried it?" one dude explained.

Hassan wasn't trying to hear them. He already knew Kim was feeling him. Hassan left out of the spot and waited outside for Kim to come out.

When Kim walked in the office Luke was on the phone. He looked up, "hey let me call you back my baby girl just walked." Luke put the phone down.

"Hey Ki Ki, did everything go okay?" Luke asked.

"Yes Dad. Ms. Carter sent you food and she wants you to put these numbers in. Oh and these cigarettes is yours," Kim said as she placed the plate of food and cigarettes down on her father's desk. Luke smiled "that lady is something else," he said as he sighed. Kim gave her father a look. Luke stopped smiling.

"Tanya went with you?" he asked.

"Yes," Kim answered.

"Okay here's six hundred give Tanya three out of it. Thanks baby girl. I'm waiting for your brothers to come they went to Queens for me.

I'll see you later you know I don't like you around here with these thirsty niggas," Luke said.

Kim shook her head, "See you Dad."

**

Kim was walking to her car when she saw Tanya standing outside talking to some dude. Kim couldn't see who it was. Tanya had a big smile on her face "there she goes"

Tanya said. When the guy turned around Kim stopped in her tracks. *Nah, it can't be him,* she thought. "Hey Kim. How are you?" Hassan asked. Kim's mouth was opened wide. "Helloooo, you lost your voice?" Hassan teased. Kim snapped out of it. "I'm good Hassan. When you came home?" she asked.

"A couple of weeks ago. I have been thinking about you from that night in Afrika House, thinking about that dance," he admitted.

Kim felt her face get red from embarrassment. "Maybe we can finish where we left off," he said. Kim's heart started racing. *Oh my God! He's home, my future baby daddy,* Kim thought. Kim laughed the question off. "Let me get your number. I'll call you later," Hassan said.

Kim gave him the number. "Kim why you still out here?" Luke asked.

"I'm leaving now Dad. Call me later Hasan," Kim said. She jumped in the car. She was smiling from ear to ear. She looked at Tanya. "What I'm gonna do T?" Kim asked.

"Girl I don't know" Tanya said honestly.

Even though Kim wanted Hassan, she was in love with Tyreek and she wasn't trying to mess that up. "I'm staying with my Reek," Kim said.

"Then so be it girl," Tanya said, "now let's go back to my moms I need to smoke. Our mission is done."

"Yea, let's roll out," Kim said as she drove off.

Easy Access

"Okay Santos, this is a piece a cake. The window is half way open. You're small enough to get through. As soon as you get in look to your right, you're gonna see the wires for the alarm and cameras. Make sure you cut both wires," Quincy instructed.

"Got it boss. Got it boss" Santos repeated.

"Look don't fucking say got it boss, if you don't do this shit right, I'm rocking your ass to sleep. I've been staking this place out for months. Now after you cut the wires open the door so Henry can come in. Y'all both collect everything you can in three minutes. Pass to me from the window and then get the fuck out. We will meet at the Honey Comb Out. Y'all got it?" Quincy asked Santos and Henry. "Nigga stop asking me dumb shit! I'm used to this let's get this money and be out. One of my shorties is waiting for me," Henry said.

"Nigga, shut the fuck up," Quincy yelled, "Santos go in!" Santos slid his skinny ass body through the window. He looked to the right and cut the wires. He then ran to unlock the door. Henry rushed in and broke the glass cases. Santos grabbed what he could. Henry took all the diamond rings, earrings and chains. Santos grabbed the rest. Henry went to the back office and took the money that was in the drawer in a zip lock bag. When he came out of the office Santos's ass was smoking his crack pipe. "WHAT THE FUCK YOU DOING?" Henry screamed. "I needed a smoke break," Santos said. "Nigga let's fucking go! Get the shit! We have less than a minute!" Santos grabbed the jewelry and then gave it to Henry.

Henry pushed the bags out the window. He began to walk towards the door. He told Santos to hurry and go out the window. Henry walked out the door and turned the corner with no problem. Quincy was in the back waiting for Santos to come out. "What the fuck is this nigga doing?" When Quincy looked in the window Santos was in there smoking his pipe. "Yo! Come the fuck on! The store opens in five minutes." Santos walked to the window.

When he got half way out someone grabbed his foot. He turned around it was the store's owner. "Oh shit Q! This nigga got my leg!" Santos shouted as he kicked the owner in his face and jumped out the window. Him and Quincy ran down the alley and came out the building. Henry was waiting with the car running; when they jumped in the car Henry sped off. "Yo! What the fuck took y'all so long," Henry questioned. "This motherfucker in the fucking store smoking his fucking crack pipe. The owner caught him leaving out and tried to grab him back inside!" Quincy said.

Henry gave Santos a look, "yo, you fucking with my money. Nigga when we on a job leave that crack shit at home. Next time, I'm gonna knock you the fuck out," Henry said. "Nigga shut the fuck up! You ain't running your brother is. Y'all niggas need me. So nigga suck my dick with all that tough talk." Henry looked at Santos like this nigga lost his mind. Henry pulled in an alleyway and stopped the car. "Nigga what you said to me?" Henry asked while pulling out his .45. "You heard what I said. I said suck... my..." In a matter of seconds Henry let off two bullets into Santos head. "Nigga you think you can talk to me like that!"

Quincy looked at Henry like he was crazy. Blood splattered all over them. "WHAT THE FUCK MAN!!" Quincy yelled, "why the fuck you did that?" "Fuck you mean? NOBODY talks reckless to me, especially no crack head. This your fault Q. you wanna get a fucking custy to come on a job with us. Now pull this nigga body out my car so we can get the fuck out of here! Hurry up!" Quincy looked at Henry in shock; he never knew his brother had it in him.

Quincy pulled Santos's lifeless body out of the car and left it in the alley. Henry and Quincy drove in silence. Henry passed Quincy some paper towel to wipe the blood off of him. "I'll make Keith clean the car as soon as we get back around the way. While he's doing that let's go to the spot and count this up." Quincy and Henry got to the hideout to count the items. In the house Quincy and Henry had so much shit from different jobs that they could have opened their own stores.

After counting up everything. They came off with sixty thousand cash and jewels. "I'm gonna give Kim and Diamond some studs," Henry said. "Yea, I'll give Kim this tennis bracelet since I didn't get her anything for her graduation," Quincy said. "Well, let's hurry up and put this shit up. I wanna go to the city to get an outfit and kicks for Travis's party. That shit gonna be poppin tonight," Henry said.
"I need some shit too. We will use my car since yours is getting cleaned then we can stop by Dexter's Barber Shop for a haircut," Quincy instructed.
**

They went to the city, picked their outfits and kicks and then went by Dexter's. When they walked in the whole team was in there, including Travis. He was sitting in the chair getting his haircut. "Well if it ain't the birthday boy. You ready for tonight my nigga?" Quincy asked. "You know it"

Travis said. Travis was one of Quincy's little goonies, he lived on Ocean Ave. He used to hang by the embassy. Travis was the youngest out of the crew but the way he carried himself you would think differently. That little niggah was fucking with grown ass women and they didn't care because he was getting that money and taking care of them.

"So do we have the V.I.P section locked down already? All of y'all got the money together?" Everybody nodded or said yes. "Good, I have to make sure my youngin birthday is right. The whole Flatbush will be out tonight. I know Mike and his team from Regent will be there. Jackie and her girls from Newkirk got a section too. I know Funk Master Flex has some surprise guest but I don't Know who it is," Quincy said. Travis was getting hype. "Yo, where the dice at?" Henry asked, "Let's get it poppin while I wait for this haircut.

**

Kim and Tanya walked in Shear Perfection as always, that shit was packed. The bitches in here could do some hair. The owner, Cleo, was at the front desk. "Good Morning ladies," Cleo said, "who y'all came for?"
"Suzette," Tanya said.

"Well she's running late but let me get one of the girls to wash y'all hair and blow dry it so when she comes in all she has to do is style it." "Thanks Cleo," Kim said.

Suzette walked in forty five minutes later and she had five bitches waiting for her. "Good Morning Bitches," Suzette walked in and greeted the ladies. "Good Morning? Bitch it's twelve noon," Cleo said, "you have five clients Tanya and Kim are first."

Suzette turned to the girls and asked what hairstyle they were getting. Kim decided to go with a high ponytail and Tanya decided to go with a Chinese bob cut. "Ok Kim let me start you first cause that's one, two, three then I got you next," Suzette said she turned towards Tanya.

Kim sat in her chair and she began to work on hair. "Are y'all going to Travis party tonight at The Tunnel?" Kim asked. "Of course, I'm going with Jackie from Newkirk," Cleo replied.

"Sue who you going with?" Tanya asked.

"I don't know. Can I roll with y'all?" she asked.

"Sure. It's only me and Kim. We in Tyreek's V.I.P section," Tanya said.

"What Tyreek?" Cleo asked.

"From the east," Kim said.

Suzette and Cleo looked at each other. Kim peeped the eye motion in the mirror. "What's all that for?" Kim asked with an attitude. "Oh nothing, we didn't know you knew him like that," Cleo replied. "That's Kim's man," Tanya said. Kim looked at Tanya with a serious look. She didn't want them to know her business plus she wanted to get information from them. "For real?" Suzette asked.

"Yes, well something like that," Kim said, "well anyways, if you wanna roll with us you can. I'll pick you up at ten thirty. So be ready."

For the next hour the girls were silent. Suzette finished both of their hair. "Alright ladies, we'll see y'all later. Sue, I'll call you ten minutes before and have a spliff ready when we come," Tanya said. Suzette laughed, "I got you T."

They left out of the shop. Cleo looked at Suzette, "why you didn't tell Kim about Ty? You know he don't have it all." Suzette looked at Cleo and said, "did you see how she was about to flip just cause I looked at you? I'll tell her tonight while we're in the car."

**

Kim and Tanya went to La Cabana to get some food. The girls ordered their food and was just sitting, waiting and talking. Just then Hassan walked in the door with one of his mans. Kim began to smile.

Hassan walked over to them, "what's good Ma" he said, "what y'all doing in here?"

"What you think?" Tanya said with an attitude, "getting some food."

"Oh ok, my bad Shorty," Hassan said to Tanya. Hassan turned to Kim and said I been thinking about you a lot!"

"Is that right?" Kim asked,

"Yes, that right," Hassan smiled and Kim's heart just melted. He had the prettiest teeth with dimples.

Just then Kim's phone rang, it was Tyreek but she didn't answer. "Who was that? Your man?" he asked. Kim looked at the phone then at Hassan. "Actually that was," she said. Hassan gave a smirk then a smile, "not for long. I'm back. I'll give you time to break up with him."

"Yo Ha, we gotta go," his man said. Kim just looked at him.

"I'll call you later Ma," he said as he walked out the door.

"Girl, what you gonna do?" Tanya asked, "Hassan is not giving up."

"I know," Kim said.

Damn, Kim thought. She thought about Hassan from time to time but Ty came in the picture. The girls got their food and got in the car. "Stop on Regent. Let me go in cabbage and get a philly blunt." Kim pulled up and as always, the block was crowded. Niggas always gambled over there. Tanya jumped out and went in the store when she came out Mike called her "YO T! Come for a second."

"What's good Mike."

"When's the last time you spoke to Latrell?" he asked.

"It's been a minute. Why?" she asked.

"I think you need to holla at him," Mike said.

"For what? He moved on, he got his girl," Tanya said.

"Look, all I'm saying is reach out to him. I can't tell you anything more. See you later," he said.

"Yea whatever, see you later."

Why must I call him when he's the one who left me? Fuck that nigga! Tanya thought. Tanya got back in the car. Kim was on the phone. "Yes, Babe," she said into the phone.

"Are you ready for tonight?" Tyreek asked.

"Yes I got all my things by Tanya," Kim replied.

"Ok, I can't wait to see you," Tyreek said, "but I'm taking care of something so I'm gone call you back."

"Ok Babe" Kim said and hung up.

Tyreek hung up the phone. "Everything is a go. I better get all my money," he said to a girl sitting next to him.

"Relax!" the girl said, "You gone get it after I deal with this bitch."

A Night to Remember

Quincy and his crew were four cars deep. Henry, Travis and Lou were in the car with Quincy. Everybody was dressed to death Quincy had on a Coogi with dark Guess jeans with some black Gucci sneakers. He wore his Cartier glasses. Henry wore a Ralph Lauren jean suit with some Jordan's. Travis had on leather pants with an iceberg sweater and some Gucci sneakers and Lou had on a Guess jean outfit with some uptowns.

"Lou roll that spliff up" Travis said.

"I got you, yo; y'all heard they found Santos's body in the alleyway by the jungle?" Lou said excitedly.

"WORD?" Travis asked.

"Yea, they said another crackhead was in the alley and saw when they dropped his body. The police want him to identify the car or the person but he was too high to remember anything clearly."

Quincy and Henry looked at each other. "That's crazy," Quincy said, "that nigga was a good dude."

"Yup," Henry added.

"I can't wait to get to this club and pop some bottles," Travis said. Henry looked at him and said, "We almost there."

**

"What's taking this bitch so long? Kim call Suzette," Tanya was getting upset. She wanted to go to the club already. Kim called Suzette. "Girl, what are you doing? We about to leave your ass! Hurry up!" Suzette ran out of the building and jumped in the car. "I don't know why y'all getting upset. Y'all know I'm never on time," Suzette said. "Next time we gonna leave your ass," Tanya said while rolling her eyes, "anyways… my gyal you look good," Tanya said with her Jamaican accent. "Thanx my fren," Suzette said. Suzette was Jamaican as well. She wore a black lace body suit with some red pumps. Her hair was in a short blonde bob.

"Yo, I can't wait to get to this club Ray supposed to meet me there. He said it's time for me to come home," Tanya said. The girls jumped on the FDR and were at the club in no time. "Damn, this shit is crowded," Kim said. Brooklyn was deep tonight. Kim seen a couple of people on the line she knew. The Westbury crew was out there. She saw Guyanese Nicky from Church Avenue walking in. Quincy and his team just pulled up to valet parking. *I'm about to do the same thing,* Kim thought. She didn't have time to look for parking.

As they were driving up to valet Suzette blurted out "Ain't that Tyreek with a bitch?" Kim pressed the brakes so hard that she almost hit somebody. It was Tyreek but she couldn't see who he was talking to. Kim pulled her phone out and called him. Tyreek looked at his phone, looked around then answered. "What's up?" Tyreek said.

"That's how you pick up your phone when you call or when you talk to other bitches in the street," Kim said. Ty laughed, "Don't start no shit." Tyreek walked away from the girl, "what's up Babe? Where you at? I'm in front waiting for you," Tyreek said.

"I'm by valet parking," Kim responded.

"Ok, I'm walking to you now."

**

"Kim can I tell you something?" Suzette asked.

"Sure Sue. What's up?" Kim asked.

"Look, be careful with Tyreek I heard stories about him. Like the nigga don't have it all. He put his hands on his bitches. I heard he even stabbed one of them."

Kim looked at Suzette and didn't believe shit that she just heard. *I hate these hating ass bitches. You can't tell them you have a man. They will do anything to break y'all,* Kim thought. "Word? I never heard that but I'll keep that in mind. Plus I don't think that nigga that crazy he knows who the fuck my brothers are," Kim stated.

"Okay girl, just giving a heads up. Be careful with that nigga," Suzette said in a concerned voice.

"Got you Sue," Kim said.

The girls met up with Tyreek and security walked them into their V.I.P section. "YO Quincy," Travis said, "Ain't that your sister over there with Tyreek and his crew?" Quincy looked over and instantly got tight. Quincy walked over to their section. "KIM!" Quincy yelled. Kim looked at him with fear in her eyes but played it off. "What's up Bro?" Kim said. "Don't fucking what's up me. What you doing over here with these niggas?"

"Relax bro, don't do that we chilling."

Tyreek walked over, "what's good Q," he said. "Why the fuck you with my sister?" Quincy asked.

"Look Q... I don't want any beef. Me and Kim have been kicking it for a minute. I like your sister. I will never violate her. I respect you and Henry too much."

Quincy looked at him. "My nigga don't fuck around." Quincy grabbed Kim's arm and pulled her to the side. "If this nigga get out of pocket you better let me know. I don't trust him," he whispered.

"Oh my God, you don't trust nobody I talk to," Kim complained.

"Cause I know these niggas. You don't! Look, enjoy your night celebrate your graduation. Me and Henry got you some gifts we gone give them to you tomorrow. Come to my table and get two bottles for you and T."

"Thanks bro. Oh, and please don't tell Dad I was here. I told him I'm staying by Tanya," Kim said.

"I got you," Quincy replied."

Kim turned to Tyreek and said, "I'll be back." Tyreek nodded his head. Once Kim walked away he screwed his face up, "bitch ass nigga," he whispered to himself about Quincy.

"Yo T, I don't trust Ty with Kim," Suzette said.

"Girl that nigga ain't crazy you didn't see how Quincy just put fear in that nigga heart," Tanya said over the loud music.

"I'm just saying," Sue said, "girl let's just party."

**

Kim walked to her brother's section. "Hey guys," Kim said. Everybody greeted her. "Everything good?" Henry asked Q.

"Yea just let that nigga know I will break his face if he fucks with my little sister," Q said.

125

"Happy Birthday Trav. You got the whole Flatbush out here," Kim said.

"Thanks. Yea you know the kid had to do it," Travis said laughing. "Well, enjoy your birthday. I'll see y'all later," Kim walked back to their section. On the way back she saw Jackie and Cleo in their section waving hello. She walked past Ahkeem, Andre and Cife from Clarkson Ave and Lenox was doing it up in their section. Kim gave Tanya and Suzette a bottle each. Tyreek bought him and her bottles so she was good.

The party was jumping, Fuck Master Flex was rocking. Just then Biggie Smalls came on stage and rocked it. When the beat dropped the whole crowd went crazy.

Who the fuck is this?
paging me at 5:46 in the morning
crack a dawn and
now I'm yawning, wipe the cold out my eye
see who's this paging me and why
It's my nigga Pop from the barbershop
told me he was in the gambling spot and heard the intricate
plot
of niggas wanna stick me like fly paper neighbor

slow down love please chill drop the caper
"Remember them niggas from the hill
up in Brownsville
that you rolled dice with
smoked blunts and got nice with?"
yeah my nigga Fame up in Prospect
nah them my niggas nah love wouldn't disrespect

Biggie was rocking with Junior Mafia. When Tanya looked on stage she saw Ray and his Seth Low Crew. *Look at my baby,* she thought, *I'm ready to, go home I miss him.* The liquor was kicking in. "Kim I'm out. I see Ray," Tanya said.

"Babe, give Tanya your car. You're driving with me," Tyreek said.

"I can drive my car Ty. I'll just drive behind you," Kim said.

"No, I want you by my side," Ty said then gave Kim a kiss, "I already have the key to the room. Here's your key."

Kim took the key. Her heart started racing. She couldn't believe tonight was the night.

"Tanya, drive my car home. I'm gonna go in Ty's car. We're going to The Riviera on Atlantic. Here's my room number just in case," Kim said.

"Girl, stop all of that being scared. Go have fun," Tanya said.

"Bitch I'm gonna text you the info. Now let's continue to party before we leave."

**

The party was off the chain. Everybody was feeling nice. The birthday boy was dancing with some chick like he was falling in love. Quincy's phone kept going off, "why my mother keep calling me? Let me text her and tell her I'm at a party," he said to himself. Travis was still dancing with the girl. Henry had some chick in the corner feeling her up. Quincy's phone kept going off. "HELLO, Ma I'm in the club I can't hear you! What? Who? When?" Quincy was asking his mother a thousand questions. "Okay, okay stop crying. I'm coming!" he said and then hung up his phone. "Yo Henry, we got to go, Dad spot got raided. He got locked, Ma just called."

As soon as they were about to leave a fight broke out. When Henry looked it was Travis fighting some big ass nigga. "YO THAT'S TRAV" Henry screamed. The whole team ran to the dance floor and began to whip these niggas ass. It turned out to be one big brawl. Tyreek grabbed Kim and walked her out of the door. Tanya and Suzette were right behind them. It turned out that Travis was dancing with some nigga girl in the club. That is what led to the brawl.

"Look, have Tanya drop you off at the hotel. I will be right behind you I swear," Tyreek said, "I have to make sure my peoples are good."

Kim went to the valet parking with Tanya. Suzette caught a ride with one of her shorties.

"I guess dreams do come true" Hassan said. Kim turned around and smiled. "Oh really?" Kim asked.

"I wished on a star that I would see you tonight and here you are." Hassan explained. Kim blushed. "I saw you in there doing your thing. So Ty is your man huh?" Hassan asked. "Yes why?" Kim asked, "It seemed like everybody has something to say."

"Nothing, nothing just be careful Ma. But you won't be with him for long. I'm coming for what belongs to me," Hassan said. Kim looked at him and said "and what's that Hassan?"

He looked her in her eyes, grabbed her hand, and said "You" and then he walked away. Kim was stuck on stupid. "Hello Kim. Let's go before you get your ass kicked," Tanya yelled. Kim got in the car. Tanya was in front of the hotel in no time. She wanted to go to Ray, she was missing him. Kim called Ty's phone. At first he didn't answer, finally he picked up. "Yes Babe, I'm right behind you."

Ty got out of a car but she couldn't see who dropped him off. "Ok T, you got the information?" Kim asked nervously.

"Bitch go and enjoy yourself. Go get some dick finally," Tanya joked as she pulled away.

**

The hotel wasn't great but it was decent. Kim sat on the bed. She was real quiet. "Are you okay?" Tyreek asked "Yes, just a little bit nervous," Kim said. "Relax Babe. I got us some champagne. Would you like some?"

"Sure," Kim said.

She was thinking about her and Tanya's conversation. *I must go with the flow. I'm gonna go change my clothes and get comfortable,* Kim thought so she went into the bathroom.

Tyreek slipped a little blue pill into her drink. *This should make her feel high,* he thought as he stirred his finger in her cup. Kim came out of the bathroom wearing lace lingerie. Tyreek's mouth dropped. *Damn, she's so pretty,* he thought to himself. He was starting to feel a little bit bad for what was about to happen to her. Kim grabbed the glass of champagne and drank it real fast. She lay down on the bed next to Tyreek. He began to rub all over her body. Kim began to moan as he kissed on her neck. He started rubbing on her G-spot. "Damn, this feel so good Ty, I have to tell you something," Kim said.

"What Babe?" he asked in-between kisses.

"I never had sex before," Kim said.

Ty stopped rubbing on her and looked her in the eyes. "Are you sure you wanna do this?" He asked.

"Yes, yes. Please don't stop."

Ty began to penetrate and her moans became louder. Tyreek felt like he was in heaven. *Damn, this pussy good. Why she had to be a job?* He thought. Kim started to feel dizzy, the room was spinning. She thought she drank too much. "Babe stop. I'm not feeling good the room is spinning." Ty didn't listen he just kept fucking her.

He turned her on her stomach and started giving her back shots. "Ty stop! Something's wrong, my eyes are blurry I can't see!" He kept on going Kim began to cry and beg him to stop. "I'm coming! I'm coming!" Ty exploded in Kim with no care. Kim lay on the bed still crying. "Something is wrong I can't-"

"Shut the fuck up with that crying!" Tyreek cut her off by screaming at her.

"Ms. Tuff girl crying now?" Kim heard a girl's voice all of a sudden. "Ty? Where are you?" Kim cried. "Here Ty. Your job is done. Here's your three gee's," the girl said.

"Thanks Steph," Ty said before he walked over to Kim and kissed her on her forehead, "it's been real Babe. Don't take it personal. It was just business for me."

Kim was in shock. "HOW CAN YOU DO THIS TO ME I TRUSTED YOU!!" she screamed.

"Listen, money over bitches any day, but let me just say you got some good pussy. Thank you for letting me hit it first," Ty said while walking out of the door. Kim cried. "TY… TY…." she called out. Kim felt a blow to the head with a bat. "Shut up bitch!" Stephanie said, "You weren't doing all this crying when you were poppin shit at my job. Remember that?"

It took Kim awhile to realize who she was. "Bitch what you want?" Kim asked as she cried. "Oh what I want? To give you what you deserve!" Another female voice appeared. "Fuck her up already Steph!" Stephanie grabbed Kim by her hair. She dragged Kim off of the bed and onto the floor. Stephanie and the other girl began to stomp on her and hit her with bats. Kim tried to fight back but she was too weak from the drug that Ty gave her. Kim felt a burning sensation on her face several times. They was kicking and stomping her out. Stephanie grabbed Kim's hair and cut it with scissors. "You think you so pretty bitch! Let's see if you think you're pretty after I finish with you!"

Kim was becoming more and more weak, she was losing blood. Stephanie cut Kim several times from her face to her arms and legs. They kept hitting Kim until her body stopped moving. "Steph, enough!" Her friend said, "She's not moving." Stephanie kicked Kim's stiff body. "Oh shit! She's dead. We gotta get out of here." Steph grabbed her things and left. Kim's lifeless body was all bruised and cut up. Her pretty face was swollen. Blood was everywhere. Kim was beat so badly. What was supposed to be a great night became her worst nightmare.

**

Quincy kept calling Kim's phone and got no answer. "Where the fuck is she?" he whispered. He called Tanya's phone several times but she didn't answered either. Luke's spot got raided and the police took him in. Their mother was crying out of control. Quincy and Henry didn't know what to do. They needed to go down to the courts but they needed Kim to come and stay with their mother.

"Hello," Tanya said.
"Finally you pick up," Quincy said, "T where's Kim."
"Huh? I can't hear," Tanya said.

"T wake up! It's Quincy, it's important. I need Kim. My Pops got locked. I need Kim."

Tanya jumped up, "WHAT! Mr. Luke? She's not here she's with Tyreek."

"What!!" Quincy became pissed off, "Where the fuck is he with my sister T?"

"I promised your sister I wouldn't say," Tanya explained.

"Tanya, don't fuck with me!" Quincy yelled.

"Okay they'll are at the Riviera Hotel on Atlantic. They in Room 130."

Quincy hung up the phone and then spoke directly to his brother, "Henry ride with me. Bring your peace," he said.

They got to the hotel room. When they knocked on the door they saw that it was already open. Henry pulled his .45 out and pushed the door. "Kim!" Henry yelled her name. Kim's clothes were everywhere. When they entered the room they saw Kim's naked bloody body on the floor. Henry dropped to his knees and started to cry. "Kiki, Wake up wake up" Henry repeated.

Quincy stood there in shock. He whispered "Kim, Kim," he took the sheet and covered her. He put her on his lap, "Kim wake up please." He check her pulse, she still had one. "Henry! She's still alive!" Quincy said, "Kim wake up please," Quincy cried. Kim opened her swollen eyes for a second. She looked at Quincy and said "help me," she then closed her eyes shut.

"Kim stop talking," Henry began to shake her but she wouldn't wake up. Quincy screamed "please don't die!"

The Housekeeper came, "Oh My God!" she hollered.

"Please, call the ambulance!" Quincy cried.

The lady just stood there.

"CALL THE AMBULANCE NOW!!!!!" he shouted.

THE END

Made in the USA
Monee, IL
03 December 2020